❖ *The French Lieutenant* ❖

BOOKS BY
RICHARD CHURCH
FOR BOYS AND GIRLS

Five Boys in a Cave
Down River
Dog Toby
The Bells of Rye
The White Doe
The French Lieutenant

❧ *The French Lieutenant* ❧
A Ghost Story

Richard Church

Here sleeps a Frenchman. Would I could
Grave in his language on this wood
His many virtues, grace and wit!
But then who'd read what I had writ?
Nay, when the tongues of Babel cease,
One word were all sufficient—Peace!

Walter de la Mare

The John Day Company
New York

The lines on the title page from Walter de la Mare's *Here
Sleeps a Frenchman* are quoted by kind permission of the
Literary Trustees of Walter de la Mare and the Society of
Authors as their representative.

First United States Publication 1972

Library of Congress Catalog Card Number: 71-147272
ISBN: 0-381-99853-3

Manufactured in the United States of America

10   9   8   7   6   5   4   3

❖ *Contents* ❖

*To Nicholas and Elizabeth,
and the great-grandchildren in
England, Canada, and the United
States of America*

1 ❈ *Good News* ❈

'Something has *got* to happen!' scowled Robert Bostock, leaning back from the breakfast table, and addressing himself to the whole family: his father, his mother, his sister, Jennifer, who was eleven, two years younger than himself, Michael, the small brother aged eight and known as the Tyke because he had the disposition of a lively terrier.

The father of this family lowered his newspaper and looked over his reading glasses at his elder son. He saw the untidy hair, the burly body, the general rough-and-tumble effect.

'What's biting you this time, Bob?'

It was said with a smile of patient tolerance.

'Oh, he's just bullying us, as usual,' said Jennifer, fastidiously lowering a finger of bread and butter into her boiled egg.

'Little prig,' muttered Bob.

'Now, now!' said Mrs Bostock. She had a gentle voice, but it always meant a lot. Father glanced aside at her, decided to ignore Bob's attack, and then studied the boy afresh.

'Why should something have to happen?' he inquired.

Bob's outburst of morning grievance subsided, but only into a frown.

'Oh, well,' he said, 'we go on, day after day, in this dull suburb. Nothing happens! It's getting monotonous, intolerable!' He went red in the face.

'What big words!' piped Michael, with his mouth full.

'You two,' said Mrs Bostock, reaching for her husband's coffee cup, which he was holding out in space for a refill, while he still studied his son, making up his mind to say something more.

'You ask for it, you know, my boy. You can't bully life into bringing what you want. You only rile people. That's what it is. You won't win that way!'

This roused Robert again. He was still red in the face with anger, though nobody had provoked him.

'It's always wait, wait, wait!' he said. 'Can't afford it! That's always the answer, whatever we want.'

Mrs Bostock smelled rebellion. She would not have her husband criticized, especially by his own son.

'Bob, you're old enough to understand,' she said. Her voice was still quiet. But so is a rod of steel. 'Father is not just an ordinary engineer, doing a routine job. You ought to know that we're living on one of his inventions, and the—and the—' her voice faltered into uncertainty, 'the consultations.'

John Bostock took the refilled cup, without looking at it. Coffee slopped over into the saucer. He didn't notice it.

'There you are, Bob! You see, *somebody* believes in me! In fact, I'll tell you something. Life has been dull for us all lately, because I've been at work on an idea, and it's taken all I've got. It just wouldn't work out! But I've said nothing. I've mastered it, and the patent has been applied for, months ago. They take a long time, these legal things.'

Then he added, before returning to his newspaper:

2

'You'll have to learn that, Bob. You cannot bludgeon people!'

'Bludgeon! Bludgeon!' echoed the Tyke, mouthing this new word like a meaty bone.

Bob glared at the brat angrily, but before he could retort, everybody's attention was stolen by the postman's knock, and the snap of the shutter over the box. All the world knows that sound; the voice of hope, of great expectations, sometimes of dread.

'I'll fetch them,' shouted Michael, and he followed his own voice quicker than a clap of thunder follows its lightning.

He came back slowly, with only one letter. 'I can read it, Daddy,' he said, 'it's in typewriting; as good as print.'

'Yes,' said his father. 'And when you're ready, I'd like to take a look as well. You might as well open it for me. Here, use a knife. Don't just tear the envelope. Slit it neatly.'

Michael was proud of this, and made much of the job, flourishing the knife with ceremony. His brother was not impressed.

'Don't show off, Tyke,' he said crushingly.

But Michael ignored this rebuke, and after his own fashion slit the envelope, withdrew the letter, unfolded it, and handed it to his father on a plate which he had snatched from the table.

'Idiot! That's got marmalade on it,' cried Bob.

'Don't shout, my boy,' said Mr Bostock. He read the beginning of the long letter, then looked up with a smile. 'It makes it all the sweeter, as you will hear, Mrs Bostock and starving family!'

He wiped the back of the letter with his napkin, and read on.

3

'What is it, dear?' said his wife. 'Does it need sweetening?'

She knew that it contained good news. One glance at her husband's eyes was enough. They shone with triumph, and for a second he looked as young as Michael. 'It's through, my love,' he said.

Mrs Bostock's eyes were moist.

'And . . .' she began, half frightened.

'You're quite right, Mary. It's exactly what you said.'

'But she hasn't!' Bob exclaimed.

His father looked at him as though he didn't exist; then he returned to the letter.

'Yes. The patent's through, and the manufacture can go ahead. Everything has been set for months past. The trade have been confident all along. A sum down and a generous royalty on sales.'

Mrs Bostock's eyes were more than moist. Tears of relief, of happiness, overflowed. Jennifer caught the infection, and wept also. She left her place at the table and ran round to clasp her mother.

'Mummy, don't, don't,' she sobbed, not knowing what it was all about.

'There, dear,' said her mother, quickly controlling herself. 'It's only the good news, after all the pinching and scraping.'

'And the long wait,' said Mr Bostock, without pausing from his further reading of the long letter, with its paragraph after paragraph about technical details; the sort of thing that professional men love, even though it may hold up proceedings indefinitely, and drive their womenfolk and their children, mad with fear that nothing may actually get done.

But Mary Bostock in tears was so unusual a sight that even Bob was disturbed, and showed it.

4

'Oh, Lord!' he said. 'Don't do it, Mother!' Then he turned impatiently on his father. 'What's it mean, Dad?'

'Yes, what's it mean, Daddy?' echoed Michael.

'If the ladies will control their emotion, I will tell you,' said Mr Bostock, who had reached the end of the letter. He looked around the table, his face like the rising sun, warm and bright, through its usual cloud of thoughtfulness. He wasn't an anxious man, for he believed in himself, though he kept quiet about it. That was why Mrs Bostock, and through her the children, had been able to remain patiently in the dreary suburban villa with its garden the size of a pocket handkerchief, and no outlook in any direction; not that an outlook would have been much consolation, for a family too poor to take advantage of it.

It is not surprising that Bob was rebellious, and had cried out that something must be done. But he was thinking about himself, and the things he wanted and could not have. He was looking at his mother now, quite angrily, since she and Jennifer were holding up the explanations, while his father sat staring at them in dismay.

But Mr Bostock quickly recovered. He was like that; his mind could take great leaps in the dark, and solve problems by the light of instinct. He knew at once what those tears meant: the long struggle with housekeeping, no regular money coming in, skimping for the home and the family.

'It means, ladies and gentlemen,' said Mr Bostock, rising from the table and clasping the lapels of his rather shabby coat, in imitation of a person making a pompous speech, 'it means that we will now seek a country retreat, a minor rural manor house with twenty bedrooms, a trout stream, a forest, and good moorlands for

5

shooting. There we will retire from this wicked and sordid world, and live happily ever after.'

'Oh, God!' said Bob.

'Oh, God!' piped Michael, again echoing his formidable big brother, except that his exclamation had left the surliness behind, and sounded cherubic.

2 ✤ *When the Pie Was Opened* ✤

Of course Mr Bostock was joking about the 'manor house with twenty bedrooms'. Perhaps he should not have taken such poetic license, for he was an inventor of gadgets to improve machinery, and not a poet who invents images to enlarge the human imagination. He must have been more excited than he appeared to be, that morning when the good news came.

For weeks nothing happened, and Bob's angry demand which preceded that news appeared to be wasted. His temper therefore did not mend. What was more odd was that Mrs Bostock lost her calm air of cheerful patience, and became quite testy, a not uncommon condition when good fortune overtakes people and threatens to alter their way of life.

Mr Bostock was away, sometimes overnight, busy at the factory where the prototype of his invention was being put into production. The gadget was some simple device for adding to machines in great industrial plants and cutting down the cost of mass manufacture by so much percent and also increasing the safety of the workers and the life of the machines.

All that was man's work, and Mr Bostock tried in vain to explain it to his wife, for he wanted her to share in all his ideas, some of them wild and theoretical, others, such as the new one, down to earth and practical.

It was also profitable, which mattered at this stage in the history of the Bostock family. For the lack of evidence of change was only superficial. Much was going on behind the daily routine, and even that monotony showed promise of greater changes to come. Mrs Bostock, so long resigned to 'make and mend', took Jennifer and Michael out one Saturday afternoon, while Bob was playing football at school. They returned with large parcels of smart new clothes; frocks for Jennifer and a suit for Michael, with shoes for both.

When Bob came home, muddy and hungry, he saw these treasures displayed on the dining-room table. He eyed them like a bull glaring at a red rag.

'No tea ready?' he demanded.

'It's in the kitchen, Bob dear,' said his mother sweetly.

'What do I get out of this?' he said.

Mrs Bostock looked at him in dismay.

'Bob, what has come over you? We can't do everything at once. I can't buy clothes for a big fellow like you unless you are with me. Your turn will come, if you're interested.'

'Oh,' he said, somewhat mollified.

'Put your muddy things in the scullery, and then we'll have tea.'

He did not bother to look at the meal laid on the kitchen table, as he blundered through to the scullery. But when he came in again, he saw a large Melton Mowbray pork pie set in the middle.

'What's that?' he asked.

The two younger children, already seated at the table, broke into laughter, yelping like two excited puppies, or so it sounded to Robert. He suspected they were scoring over him.

'Stop that row!' he growled.

8

'Robert, please!' said his mother. 'What makes you behave like that? We're all excited. This is to celebrate. And it's to please you, because we could not leave you out when we were shopping.'

'What is there to celebrate?' he asked, a little more amiably.

'I'll tell you,' said Mrs Bostock. 'I can do so now that we are certain. Father and I have said nothing because we were afraid of raising false hopes. But it's like this . . .'

She paused, to give her full attention to cutting three equal segments of pork pie. Lumps of delicious jelly oozed round the knife.

'Ho! Ho!' moaned Michael, in an ecstasy of anticipation. He had never before eaten a pork pie, and this meant more to him at that moment than manor houses in the country with twenty bedrooms.

The other two, Jennifer and Bob, were more divided in their attention. Being older than Michael, they saw further ahead, and could think of two things at once.

'Go on, Mother, we're waiting!' exclaimed Bob.

'Yes,' she said, 'well, as I was saying . . .' She balanced one slice of pie on the knife and slid it onto a plate, which she passed to Bob.

'You see, the firm who make the machinery which Father's invention has improved is a very big concern, and . . .'

She paused again, to deal with the second slice of pie, which Michael tried to grab. But she pushed his hand back, and looked at him severely. Then she put the plate in front of Jennifer, who at once attacked it, guardedly watching the small brother sitting beside her at the table. But she was also attentive to her mother's interrupted story.

9

'Well, the head of that firm is, of course, a very rich man, and he lives in an old castle in the country.'

She paused again, to deal with Michael's portion. Then she cut a tiny piece for herself, and took a mouthful. 'Ah,' she said, 'this is no pie in the sky!'

The children did not even hear this. Michael was head down over the short crust, the succulent pork and the golden jelly. Bob and Jennifer were savouring the novelty also but waiting for further facts, and no nonsense.

'If I were rich, I wouldn't have an old castle. I'd have a new one,' said Jennifer.

'Don't speak with your mouth full,' said Bob. His plate was empty, and he held it out to his mother.

'No, Bob. Pork pie is very rich, too, and your stomach isn't used to it. Cut some bread!'

He glared at her, but obeyed, and tried to be grown-up.

'Well, what comes next?' he asked.

'They are so pleased with Father, all those directors, that they can't do too much to help him. There's a big estate round the castle, with farms. One of the farmhouses is as old as the castle, and it is empty because two farms have been modernized and merged into one.'

That information interested nobody. It produced not even a sigh of impatience. Bob and Jennifer just waited. Michael was still alone in the world with his dwindling portion of pie.

'You were saying . . .' It was Bob, quite polite for once.

'Well, the chairman has offered us this old farmhouse, and a big garden round it, a walled garden where we can grow our own vegetables, and a flower garden, too. Just think of it, children! Just think of it!'

Jennifer interrupted, to damp her mother's enthusiasm.

'But if it's a very old farmhouse, won't it tumble down?'

'No, dear. It's got walls three feet thick, and wide window-seats. Father has been down to see it, and the estate workmen are doing it up for us, inside and out. Oh, you can't imagine!'

Perhaps the small slice of pork pie had brought some color to Mrs Bostock's face, which had looked pale and tired for months past. Her eyes were bright, too, instead of being dull and resigned behind their veil of patience, which had been wearing thin.

That was how Mr Bostock saw her as he came in. Nobody at the table had heard his key, or the closing of the front door. They were too excited. He noticed his wife, untidy, flushed and very pretty again.

'You've been out on the spree!' he said, bending to kiss her hair. 'What's this? Pork pie! Why, that's what we used to call high tea, ages ago. Now I'll take a slice of that, if you please, and Mother and I will sip at a glass of dry sherry with it, if our children don't mind.'

'We don't mind!' shouted Jennifer and Michael, infected by the overflow of parental happiness. But Jennifer had an afterthought.

'Why do you call it *dry* sherry, Daddy, when it's wet?'

'Ah! That is a difficult question. I must have further notice of that!'

Father joined them at the table, and the little kitchen was crowded with an excited family, all talking at once, with Mrs Bostock so distracted that she did not notice that Bob had helped himself, after his father, to another section of pork pie.

After a while, the hubbub subsided, and Mr

Bostock was able to talk without interruptions. He told the story of the offer of the old farmhouse, and said that within a month they would be able to move down to Kent, where the castle stood in its moat, hidden from main roads at the end of a mile-long drive over rising ground and into a wooded valley. The farmhouse, he said, was at the farther boundary of the estate, four miles from the castle, across fields, woods, and beyond a little river which paused at the castle to fill the moat, then flowed on northward to join a bigger stream, a tributary of the Thames.

'Marvelous!' concluded Mr Bostock. 'We shall be back in the Middle Ages!'

'What are the Middle Ages?' inquired Michael, who had finished his portion of pie and returned to the twentieth century.

'You'll see when we get there,' said his father.

'So we're moving?' cried Bob.

'We're moving, my lad!'

Mr Bostock beamed like the risen sun on his first-born, who responded with a remark that almost signified satisfaction.

'Then something is going to happen at last!'

Bob's mother looked at him, then shook her head with sadness, an emotion quite out of place amid the general excitement over the good news.

3 ❧ Moving Day ❧

The Bostock family moved in the early spring. None of them, except perhaps the mother, could have said how it was done. Think of a hurricane raging through the small suburban house, snatching the pictures from the walls and leaving bright patterns where the paper had not faded; curtains torn down and carpets torn up, rolled into dusty bundles as heavy as lead; covers stripped off chairs and mattresses off bedsteads, and all this soft furniture sent away to the cleaners for urgent delivery to the still imaginary house which the children had not yet seen, and therefore could hardly believe it really existed.

There followed several days of living, or rather camping, in the half-naked villa, with picnic meals and everybody in everybody else's way, and nobody caring about the discomfort, and the hollow noise of voices clashing against the naked walls.

But on moving day, when two vans drew up outside the house and threw their great shadow over it, darkening it and reducing it to a shabby relic already dismissed into the past, Mrs Bostock calmly took command as though she were an admiral aboard his flagship. The chaos and confusion retreated before her, and her orders were instantly obeyed by meek husband and docile children.

The foreman of the team that came with the vans was a wizened old character who wore a green baize apron and a cap which seemed to be part of his skull, and irremovable. He deferred to Mrs Bostock as though she were a queen, and moved his men accordingly. 'The Lady says do this,' or 'the Lady wants that,' and the team, one of whom was a giant with no powers of speech, instantly obeyed instructions.

Packing cases were brought in from the vans, and one specialist, with a pile of newspapers beside him, wrapped and packed china and glassware, and the small odds and ends which accumulate in every household without any member of the family knowing when, why, or whence. He had the gestures of a conjurer. Objects shrank in his hands, to take a minimum of space in the packing cases. Jennifer and Michael stood and watched him, hypnotized by this light-fingered magic. He appeared to be half asleep and quite unaware of the children's presence, until Jennifer suddenly offered him the doll which she had been carrying about all morning, for fear of its being left behind. He took it from her, solemnly kissed its china cheek, wrapped it up, and tucked it safely into a suitable niche.

'Bless her heart,' he said; and Jennifer believed him, and was comforted. She allowed her mother to collect her, so that she should not get in the way of the mate who was feeding cups, saucers, vases, ornaments, from all over the house, to this magician.

So the morning passed to midday, and the break for luncheon. The men had their victuals with them and settled down in the kitchen. The family went out to a drab café on the main road. A March wind blew dust and litter along the streets, and a blanket of smoky cloud across the sky, darkening the suburb.

'Ugh, it's chilly,' said Bob, who had been rather

14

depressed all the morning, in spite of the general excitement and the anticipation of what lay ahead.

'Cheer up, Bob,' said his father, over the fish and chips. 'Do you know, my boy, that you're inclined to let things turn to dust and ashes as soon as you touch them?'

'No sermons today, John, please,' said his wife. 'We're all over-excited. Who wouldn't be?'

Mr Bostock grunted. 'Huh! I don't see much excitement in Bob's face. He looks really down in the mouth.'

'Oh, Bob's always grumpy,' said Michael. 'He was born like that.' The child spoke without looking up. He was more intent on his plate of fish and chips than on the niceties and nastinesses of his brother's nature. His words were merely an aside, but they stung. Robert scowled at him, and was about to say something really violent, had not Jennifer floated one of her mothlike remarks across the table.

'You weren't there when Bob was born. You weren't even thought of.'

'I must have been waiting about somewhere,' said Michael.

'You're both talking rot,' growled Bob. He was half inclined to laugh with his parents at this sage retort from the eight-year-old.

'All we know is that we're here,' said the father. 'And tonight we'll be there. Now Jennifer's going to say that's neither here nor there, aren't you, my pet?'

Jennifer smiled blissfully. Nothing disturbed her. She flitted from twig to twig of her own tree of life like a wren.

'You know your way?' Mr Bostock asked the foreman when the family returned to find the house an empty shell. The tailboards of the vans were up and fastened.

'We go by instinct, guv'nor,' said the old gnome. 'John o' Groats to Land's End, anywhere you like to mention. You name it, we'll find it.'

'Reproved!' laughed Mr Bostock. 'You've kept one crate of beer for tonight?'

'Tonight! We'll be there in a couple of hours, and have the stuff out in a jiffy!'

'What's a jiffy?' asked Jennifer. There was more laughter, and in this mood the team with the two vans moved off, leaving the Bostock family to an uncanny silence at the front door of the empty house which was no longer their home. A half-suppressed sob broke the silence. Michael was weeping.

'I've got nowhere to live,' he cried.

Bob did not hear this, for he had gone upstairs to have a last look round. Maybe he, too, felt a touch of gloom, and did not care to let it be observed.

Mrs Bostock drew the small boy to her, and comforted him. Jennifer could look after herself, and was busy helping her father with suitcases, which had yet to be loaded into the trunk of the car.

'Robert,' shouted Mr Bostock, up the stairs. 'Come and give a hand with the luggage!' He might have been shouting in a cavern.

A minute or two later Robert came downstairs. He was pale.

'Are you all right, dear?' asked his mother.

'Of course!' he said angrily. 'We're going, aren't we?'

A cold March shower drove them without further delay into the car and, as they moved off, raindrops blurred the last view of the house, making it all the more forlorn, as though it were melting.

Everybody was silent for a while, as Mr Bostock drove slowly with the traffic out of southeast London.

'Pretty good,' he said, as they crossed Blackheath. 'A bit later and we'd have been caught up in the rush hour!'

The shower was over, and blue sky spread from the opening countryside. The sun broke through behind them, and lit up the fields, the warm brown woodlands, the slopes of the Downs. The Weald lay ahead, mile beyond mile, with its rose-red villages, its bare hop gardens where the new strings from pole to pole shone like golden wires. Oasthouses with their white-capped kilns glowed warm in the sunlight. It was another world. It was a fairyland. Already that dreary villa dissolving behind the curtain of rain was lost in the past.

The car turned more southerly, across the lower undulations of the Weald. It left the main road to the coast and wound its way more slowly round the myriad curves in the narrow byroads and lanes.

A stop was made in a rocky woodland, because Jennifer had whispered urgently into her mother's ear that she felt unwell. Mother and daughter disappeared into the wood, behind one of the great ironstone rocks.

'Well, boys, we might as well make ourselves comfortable,' said Mr Bostock. 'Don't wander away now!'

Bob trod down the undergrowth: dead stuff with a few shoots of new life on vicious-looking bramble boughs, young green, feathery plants which the town-bred boy neither knew nor noticed. But he heard the voice of a thrush. It shouted at him, either in challenge or good cheer. And a blackbird with yellow beak rose in front of him, scolding loudly.

He realized that, otherwise, he was alone. It was a strange sensation. He felt small, and this did not please him. He turned and hurried back to the car, but he must have lingered, for he found the rest of the family seated and impatient.

'Come on, man,' said his father sharply. 'We are all waiting.'

Robert did not apologize as the car moved off.

There was no other stop, for in midafternoon, traffic on the lanes was scarce. They passed through a village on a hill, with the stone church crowning it, set amid houses and cottages, some tile-hung, some with weatherboarded sides and others of the rose-red medieval brick.

'That's Cranehurst, our nearest metropolis,' said Mr Bostock. 'Only two miles farther, then we turn down the private lane. Keep a lookout for the house, boys. But you won't see it, yet. It's four miles along the lane, past the castle, beyond that ridge and into the valley, hidden away from the world.'

Sure enough, there was the lane on the left. The entrance dropped sharply down from the road, and Mr Bostock took the turning slowly.

'Nasty bit, that,' he said. 'Worse still getting out of it. Might as well have a portcullis to keep the twentieth century out.'

They drove in low gear, past large fields, one to the left a vivid apple-green with young wheat; that on the right bedraggled with patches of last year's thistles and dead stalks, among which a small herd of black-and-white cows stood around a huge cradle full of hay. Every head, with mournful eyes, was turned to watch the car go past.

'Now, children,' said Mr Bostock, as the car sloped into a dip where the lane was crossed by running water, 'keep your eyes open to the right, and you'll see something!'

Bob disliked being told what to do, and he shut his

eyes. Michael, who was perched on the edge of the front seat between Bob's legs, had the eyes of a lynx.

'Look! Look!' he cried, levering himself up with his hands on his brother's knees. 'What's that, Daddy? Among those trees! I can see them: two little turrets, on a big tower. And two arrows pointing different ways; what are they for?'

'Those are weathervanes, to show which way the wind blows.'

'But they show two ways.'

'Oh, well, a politician once lived there,' said Mr Bostock, following a curve in the lane, which revealed the whole of the tower and a long range of the castle.

Michael screwed himself round to appeal to his mother, who sat behind with Jennifer.

'What does Daddy mean?' he asked, but his movement had squeezed Bob's right leg and hurt it.

'Blast you, sit still!' cried Bob, as he thumped the Tyke in the ribs.

'Now stop, boys,' said their mother, leaning forward to put a restraining hand on Bob's shoulder. 'We're nearly there, so be patient. Look, Jennifer, there's the castle where the chairman lives.'

'What chairman?' Jennifer was sleepy, her wits not as sharp as they usually were.

'The head of the firm who are making Daddy's new patent.'

'He's a very sick old man,' said Mr Bostock. 'I didn't tell you that. I thought it might put you off the place.'

Mrs Bostock was inclined to feel other people's troubles overmuch. There was a family joke about it. Her husband once said that she was psychic; a remark that had to be explained, in vain, to Jennifer and Michael. It merely made Bob snort in derision, and murmur something about 'all that stuff', a remark which his father had not taken too kindly.

At this moment, however, Mrs Bostock was not affected. She was tired by the journey, after the weeks of excitement and hard work over the removal from town to country. Anticipation can make people tired, too, even if it is pleasurable and full of hope.

The bickering between the boys subsided as the car passed along the front of the castle, a long, low building pierced by a noble archway.

Mr Bostock stopped the car and pointed toward the garden beyond the archway.

'There it is. You see? The old tower and a further archway to the lower garden? It's all very old; four hundred years. Think of that, Jennifer; four hundred years, and those bricks have stood firm. Can you see the ornamental work? No? We'll come up tomorrow and have a closer look. We can walk round the gardens and explore the tower.'

'Let us get along, John dear,' pleaded Mrs Bostock from the back seat. 'We've had nearly enough for one day.'

'I said tomorrow, Mary,' he answered, as the car moved on. Tempers were somewhat frayed.

'Yes, dear, but . . .' She said no more; nor did any of the others.

They were all tired and hungry. Even when Mr Bostock suddenly exclaimed, 'There it is, straight ahead,' there was little response.

The farmhouse stood on rising ground, above another secret little valley, about four miles from the castle, which was now out of sight.

The house was approached up a short drive, over an open grass patch, half hidden behind an enormous oak-tree. A misselthrush shouted a challenge as the car halted in front of the house. He was somewhere among those bare branches, the twigs already swollen with reddish-brown bumps, the promise of buds. 'His family have been on sentry go there for four hundred years. This house was built at the same time as the castle. But we'll have the history later on!'

Mr Bostock looked at his wife, pretending to be reproachful because of her impatience when they stopped in front of the castle.

'Welcome home the Bostocks!' he said, pretending to be ceremonious by opening the car doors and taking off his cap as the family alighted. The boys scrambled out, staggering on stiffened legs for a moment, then standing side by side to stare at what lay before them.

Mrs Bostock and Jennifer joined them, and father stood behind, one hand on his wife's shoulder, and the other on Bob's.

'Well?' he said.

'Oh, John, it's not true,' said the mother.

'I'd better confess,' he spoke in a low, sepulchral tone, 'it's supposed to be haunted!'

Jennifer trembled, and hid her face in her mother's coat.

'No, Daddy, no,' her muffled voice cried.

A peal of laughter rang out from the rest of the family. The front door opened. It was a great oak affair gray with time, studded with iron nails, a huge lock, and ornamental hinges spread half across the wood.

There stood a countrywoman, smiling shyly.

'That's the right way to come,' she said. 'A good laugh to begin with! Been expecting you all afternoon, but can't do much until the furniture comes up.'

She came out and shook hands all round, then took a suitcase from the trunk, as Mr Bostock began to unload.

'Here, Bob,' he said. 'Let's make a start.'

'We've got some provisions with us,' said Mrs Bostock.

'You don't want to worry over that, ma'am,' said the countrywoman. 'My name's Kate Green, and my man works on the estate. I was told up at the castle you was coming, and I was to see you in.'

She seized a second suitcase, and drove Mrs Bostock before her past the great oak door into the hall, where she put the bags down on the flagstones. A log fire burned on the open hearth, under the great beam surmounted by a long chimney-shelf. All looked very bare, but scrubbed clean. A smell of herbs, of incense, of wood smoke, and ancient time itself, came from the fireplace, the walls, the rafters, the shallow staircase.

'I reckoned you'd be peckish after all that traipsing,' said Mrs Green. 'So I brought something up and got it ready in the kitchen. They left the old table there, you see, and there's the new electric stove. Proper palace they've made of it, ma'am.'

'Oh, that is good of you, Mrs Green.'

Mrs Bostock was so bewildered by the day's events and by relief at finding a meal prepared, that for a moment she lost her sense of command, and could find nothing more to say.

The family was summoned into the kitchen, and stood around the long scrubbed table, while Mrs Green served up a fragrant meal of eggs and bacon on plates which she had brought from her cottage.

The family ate standing.

'The Feast of the Passover,' said Mr Bostock.

'Ah, sir,' said Mrs Green, 'I see you know your Bible. That ain't so usual nowadays.'

Bob looked at her suspiciously, but at that moment the vans arrived, and all was flurry and excitement.

Mrs Green clattered the dirty plates, knives, and forks into the sink. 'I don't much hold with those contrivances,' she said to Mrs Bostock, nodding toward the newly installed dishwasher. 'But I'll just get my things out of the way so they don't get mixed up, like.'

The old foreman and his team, including the speechless giant, instantly began to unload, after first, and reverently, bringing in the crate of beer and placing it safely on the kitchen table.

'If I can be of any more help . . .?' ventured Kate Green.

'No, you've been an angel,' said Mrs Bostock, completely restored by good food and hot tea. She really wanted to be amidst her family, unembarrassed by strangers, at this moment, the beginning of a new life, in which she could still only half believe.

The team worked with the speed and precision of a squadron of artillery manning a gun. Mrs Bostock, with her husband as lieutenant, took command again, moving about the house directing the disposition of the furniture. The carpets had already arrived and had been laid. By nightfall, the old farmhouse was a home once again. The team stood round the kitchen table, and Mr Bostock joined them with two bottles of champagne. They were polite about that, and the foreman removed his cap, to reveal a completely bald head. But they returned gratefully to the beer. With friendly remarks, and a grin from the silent giant, they drove away into the darkness. The rumble of the vans diminished, then ceased.

The Bostocks stood outside, in the silence. Behind the woods farther up the lane, a full moon was rising. It could almost be seen to move, like the minute hand of a grandfather clock. The thrush in the oak tree gave **three final blasts** and then gave up.

'Well, we're here,' said Mr Bostock. 'What do you say?'

But nobody said anything. They were almost asleep on their feet.

'Shall we see the ghost, Daddy?' whispered Jennifer, after the uncanny silence had wrapped itself further and further round the family. But it was brother Bob who answered.

'Don't talk nonsense. There's no such thing,' he exclaimed, as though he had been insulted.

That broke the spell, and the Bostocks went indoors for their first night in the old farmhouse.

4 ❋ *The First Look Round* ❋

They woke next day before sunrise, roused by the din of bird-song, Nature's morning chorus. It began with a sleepy note, one here, another there, lost in the misty landscape. In the far distance a cock crowed, a lonely challenge. Somewhere, and nearer, it was answered, loud enough to rouse other voices.

Suddenly, from the great oak tree in front of the farmhouse, the misselthrush who had heralded the arrival of the newcomers started up, more triumphant than ever. He woke every kind of feathered creature. A blackbird began fluting, his long liquid notes more tuneful than the thrush's thrice-repeated themes. That set off the whole orchestra of dawn: robins, chaffinches, and tits, with an impatient chatter of sparrows and starlings.

That home thrush wakened Michael. He blinked, then opened those inquisitive eyes wide. He was a sharp one, Michael; hearing as well as seeing. Not much escaped his curiosity.

He was out of bed in a second, disturbing Robert, whose body shook with resentment, though he did not wake.

Michael clambered onto the deep window ledge, and opened the leaded casement wider. In surged the music: the cock crow, the flute, the oboe, the pizzicato of sparrows. A flight of rooks, passing over the farm-house, gave their squawking croaks like side drums.

'Shut up,' groaned Robert, still only half awake.

But Michael instantly became part of it, with his first daybreak in the country. He crowed like a cock. Then he tried to imitate the nearby tune of the thrush, with its triple repeats.

Robert sat up, rubbed his eyes, scowled at his young brother.

'Cranehurst Grammar School!' he said. 'And you, too, Tyke: some little prep school. We've got to start again. No fun, starting at a new school. Everybody down on you.' He punched the air, one fist, then the other fist. 'But I'll hold my own!'

Michael wasn't interested in this. His head was thrown back, as he sniffed the country air which his brother was punishing so savagely. It smelled of grass, of cows, of a general almondlike mixture of wild flowers.

'I'm going out!' he said, scrambling into his clothes. 'Come on, Bob!' He disappeared.

But Bob was slower. He moved heavily. Mr Bostock looked in while Bob was sorting out his shirt, vest, and trousers, which he had dumped on the floor overnight.

'What about it, son? A look round, eh? The Tyke's already gone downstairs, and Jennifer's in the kitchen. She's seeing to the breakfast, for Mother's a bit overdone after yesterday. We'll take her up a tray later on.'

'Why, is she ill?'

'Ill? Of course she's not ill. You're a tough one, I must say! Don't you realize what she's had to do over the past few weeks, with this job of moving house? D'you think the fairies did it?'

Robert ignored such talk.

'What about the new school, Dad?' he said, talking through his shirt.

'Is that worrying you? Another week to Easter, and we've agreed that you shall start with the new term after the holidays. So you're lucky, with an extra week beforehand. We shall be settled in nicely by then. Come on now, and don't seek for trouble. Let's look around outside for half an hour. You're interested, aren't you?'

Mr Bostock was puzzled by his elder son. He himself was a man full of enthusiasm and eagerness. That is what had made him an inventor, and had prevented him from staying in a routine, reliable job. Now he was at last a really successful inventor. He was on top of the world.

'Come on, old boy,' he cried. 'Let's find young Michael, or he'll beat us to it.'

Robert looked at his father with a leaden eye. 'And make all the discoveries?' he said, with a sarcastic leer.

But he followed Mr Bostock downstairs to the kitchen, where they found Jennifer setting the table for breakfast.

'You come, too, Jenny,' said her father, seizing her by the shoulders. 'Breakfast can wait, and we'll leave Mother in peace for a while. She can sleep it out until we come back to tell her what we've found.'

The early sunlight, tangled in dewy mist, flickered over Mr Bostock, who had halted outside the great oaken door. He stood with one arm round Jennifer's shoulders, the other round Robert's. He drew a deep breath, slowly exhaled, then drew another.

'This is living!' he said.

Robert squirmed from under the fatherly arm. 'What is?' he muttered.

'Why, can't you see it, smell it, hear it? Even that plane going over only adds to the triumph.'

Mr Bostock's enthusiasm affected Jennifer, and she jumped up and down, making her father stumble. Robert moved farther away, embarrassed. This broke the magic spell, and the party walked round outside the house, to the barn across the neglected lawn which was spattered with golden dandelions, buttercups, and colts-foots, over the vivid green of April's grass. Diamonds of dew caught the level sunlight, and broke it up to rain-bow colors. The dew also wet the shoes of the three explorers.

'Oh, Daddy, my slippers!' cried Jennifer.

Her father flung her up and carried her piggy-back.

'Milksop!' said Robert, slashing at a thistle skeleton with a stick which he had found. He liked weapons.

Michael came running out of the barn. The portal was so large, with its double doors gaping, that the Tyke might have been a young rabbit, he was so diminished.

'Come on! Come on!' he shouted. 'It's as big as a railway station, as big as . . . as big as . . .' but words failed him. He ran and seized his brother by the arm, urging him on; but Robert refused to hurry. The father was more understanding. 'Yes,' he cried, as excited as his younger son, 'we'll do something with this, boys. Make a wonderful workshop! Room for us all! Look, there's a ton of hay been left behind: wicked waste!'

'Perhaps the ghost eats it?' The voice came from above his head, and he looked up in surprise. He was so elated that he had forgotten the living burden on his back. Laughing, he swung Jennifer down, and the three stood at the threshold of the barn, staring in at its immensity, the enclosed emptiness in half darkness, cut by a ray of sunlight solidified by dust raised from the human footsteps.

The hay was stored on a gallery at the end, reached by an open staircase against the wall, with one hand-rail polished by years of handling.

Suddenly a young rabbit bolted from the farther corner under the balcony. Robert sprang forward, and aimed a blow with his stick as the little creature fled from the barn.

'Ah! Missed!' said Robert, and slashed at the dusty sunbeam instead. Jennifer began to cry.

'What's the matter with *you*?' demanded Robert. He was angry.

Mr Bostock and Michael comforted the girl, the father by drawing her to him, and Michael by butting her with his head.

'It's cruel! Cruel,' she sobbed, but was quickly re-assured by her father. Even so, she eyed her elder brother cautiously during the rest of the walk round the farmyard, beyond the barn, through the walled garden waist-high in last year's weeds, as far as the small mea-dow that curved back toward the garden behind the farmhouse.

'What about breakfast?' said Bob, half an hour later.

'Yes, I'm hungry and starving!' shouted Michael. 'I'm going to die if I'm not fed.'

'Pity I missed that rabbit!' growled Robert, prod-ding the comic infant with his stick.

'Come on, then,' said the father. 'I'm ravenous, too. We're all hungry, aren't we, Jenny?'

As she agreed, they raced each other back to the house, from which there floated one of the most delicious smells in the world: frying bacon and hot coffee.

'Ah! She's up!' said Mr Bostock. 'She's beaten us again!'

But nobody minded, least of all the mother who had

come downstairs immediately she heard her family leave the house. By some marvelous means known only to women, especially if they are good wives and mothers, she had made the great kitchen come to life again, and to be familiar and belonging.

The long table stood in the middle of the brick floor, the chairs waited round it. The loaves of white and brown bread brought in by Mrs Green from some as yet unknown bakery, a plate of roughly patted-up golden butter, a sizzling frying-pan on the new electric stove giving off delicious fumes of eggs and bacon, set beside the coffee pot; all awaited the eager but talkative mouths of the rest of the family who competed to tell Mother what had been seen outside the old farmhouse, and what each and every one intended to do with this newly-inherited world of wonders.

5 ❉ A Slight Scratch ❉

Mrs Green appeared at the kitchen door from the scullery before the family had finished breakfast.

'I see you found everything all right then?' she said to Mrs Bostock, who was pouring her husband's third cup of coffee. 'I reckon you knows your way about, ma'am. Looks as though we shall get on well together.'

'Why, are you able to come up regularly, Mrs Green? Oh, isn't that splendid!'

' "Kate's" good enough for me, if you please. That's how I'm called up at the castle, all my life there. Used to be plenty of staff in those days, before the war. Me dad was undergardener, and mum a housemaid. Mind you, it isn't the place it used to be in olden days, so they say; hundreds of years ago. It's had its ups and downs; but you can't believe all those old tales.'

'Tell us some of them, Mrs Green!' cried Jennifer, running to her and clasping her round the waist.

'Well, if you ain't a friendly little soul,' said the astonished Mrs Green. 'I'm not much used to such kindness. We country folk are a rough lot, y'know. We works hard, but we don't have much to say.'

'You're not doing too badly,' said Robert, over a slice of brown bread and marmalade.

'Bob!' said his mother, frowning at him.

'I must say I miss *The Times*.' This came from Mr Bostock, who was impatient of gossip. He rose from the table, still drinking his coffee. 'I must try out my new study, Mary. All those letters we brought from home yesterday, not opened yet! But what am I saying? That fusty villa in London is no longer home. *Here* is our home!' And in front of Mrs Green he flung his arms wide, walked twice round the table, pulling Michael's and Jennifer's hair, and planting a kiss on his wife's head. He did not touch Robert.

Mrs Green beamed with approval and surprise. 'Well, if that don't take some beating, for a happy family!' she said. 'But I don't want to be familiar, mind you, ma'am.'

She was so shocked by her own friendliness (it was contagious from Mr Bostock) that she retreated into shyness and the huge scullery-washhouse behind the kitchen, to pick her way amongst the confusion of bits of furniture and oddments still undisposed around the house.

'John, I can't believe it!' whispered Mrs Bostock, clutching the husband towering benevolently above her. 'Keep your fingers crossed! When did I last have help in the house?'

'What about a willing husband and three eager children, madam?'

'*Three*, did you say?'

She saw Robert look at her suspiciously, and she added quickly, 'Of course, dear, all *three* of them. And *you* do your best, when you are around.'

'Well, that won't be so frequently in the future, my lady. From now on I'm likely to be enslaved by these big business tycoons, picking my brains.'

'And paying for it, John,' she said. 'You've no head for finance, have you?'

'Ah, I know my weakness. And to know that, is to be forewarned and armed to the teeth!'

'We've heard that before,' muttered Robert.

His father looked at him, perplexed by the morose remark.

'Where do you get it from, Bob?' he said.

'Get what?'

But Mr Bostock did not explain. He left the kitchen, and the first breakfast party in the farmhouse broke up. Mrs Bostock and Jennifer cleared the table, and carried the dirty crockery to the scullery, where Mrs Green was already sorting out pails, brushes, and other household tools, so that she could set about cleaning and polishing in rooms already immaculate but dusty with straw and sacking from the incoming furniture.

The children were free. Michael and Jennifer disappeared through the back door, their cries of excitement dying away into the distance.

'Give me a hand with some of this stuff, will you, Bob?' said his mother. 'We'd best get most of it up to the attics. The odd chairs can go into the spare bedrooms. Oh, how wonderful to have some space at last!'

Mrs Green responded before Robert. She prized open a packing case with a large screwdriver, and found it to be full of books.

'Whatever!' she exclaimed. 'Just a lot o' books! That'll belong to the master, I reckon. Better go into his room, eh, ma'am?'

Mrs Bostock did not respond, because she was studying Robert. He had followed her sulkily into the scullery and stood waiting.

'Well, Bob?' she said sharply, annoyed perhaps, or even anxious at his moodiness.

'Dad leaves me out,' he complained.

'What *do* you mean? Leaves you out of what, and when?'

'It's always so. Just now, when he walked round the

table, and . . .' but he could not finish. He could not find the right words.

'Don't imagine things!' said his mother. 'We get what we give in this world.'

Robert ignored that, because he could not understand it. It was something he might have heard in his sleep.

'We must get this scullery cleared, Bob, or Mrs Green and I will be driven mad, dodging round and searching for things we can't find. We're not like you men . . .'

The puzzled frown cleared from Robert's face. His mother had called him a man. That was something he agreed with. He became quite civil, and for the next hour worked willingly with the two women, carrying and placing around the house the odd chairs and occasional tables, left in the scullery by the moving-men for lack of instruction where to put them.

'Now these suitcases: we've got rid of the things in them. Let us take them up to one of the attics, Bob. I've not been up there yet. Are they dry, and fairly clean . . . Kate?' She hesitated a little, over addressing Mrs Green so familiarly. She was afraid of sounding superior. But the good woman had asked for it, and now accepted it easily.

'Why, bless me, when there was a bailiff on the estate, running the farms, he lived here, and two maids used to sleep up in them attics. Went up a ladder through the trapdoor, they did. But the builder has put in a proper contraption now: an aluminum pair o' steps that comes down easy-like as you pull the trapdoor down, all fastened together and balanced, so a child could work it. I had a go up there last week, thinking you'd have a use for them. There are two, and quite a size

34

they are, with little old windows, been there these hundreds of years; pretty diamond panes, set in lead. Fair makes you giddy, looking out of them across country. But you can see the top of the castle tower from up there, where the hill slopes down toward the river that comes out of the moat.'

Mother and son listened entranced. Mrs Green had a gift for storytelling, because she was interested in things and people around her. She loved life, and that gave her wisdom. The Bostock family were lucky, and Mrs Bostock, who was uncommonly quick herself, already appreciated that good luck.

'Well, Kate, you lead the way. We'll all take some of this stuff not wanted on the voyage.'

Kate, who had never left the neighborhood of her birthplace, seemed not to hear Mrs Bostock's little joke.

'What about that load o' books, ma'am?'

'Oh, we must leave them for my husband to sort out. There's plenty of room on those new shelves in his study. I expect he'll want them handy.'

The three beasts of burden made their way upstairs, and along the main landing, which turned at the end to a recess, lit by a narrow window that was once an open slit in the deep outer wall. A long pole with a hook hung from a nail. Kate took it, reached up, and fixed the hook in a ring hanging from a trapdoor above. With one steady pull, as though she were ringing a church bell, she swung the trapdoor open, and the metal ladder came telescoping down.

'As easy as that,' she said. 'Up you go, young man. You be first, and we'll pass the things from below.'

Robert looked around as his head rose above the attic floor. He saw a mixture of old and new. A king post stood supported by a massive beam that stretched across the floor. It carried a vaulting of smaller beams

35

which still were seen, though the spaces between them had been filled in with modern insulating fabric, hiding the roof tiles. Two huge water tanks had been lapped with soft material that gave them the appearance of slumbering elephants. Beyond them was a tiny door that must have led to the rest of the roof beams right across the old building. The wide floor space was empty, and not clearly seen because the dormer window was small, and deep set in the thick wall.

Mrs Green must have dusted down the diamond panes, for the morning sunlight from the southeast threw a clear ray across the floor toward the little door beyond the tanks. A tattered square of brown felt lay on the irregular floorboards. Where the sunlight crossed the boards it picked out knots, and soft patches where the woodworm had fed. Old age, silence, timelessness: the atmosphere hung about the attic.

Robert clambered off the ladder and stood upright, still looking round him. He noticed that Mrs Green had not done much with the window. One pane in the middle was scratched and had the appearance of a blind eye. He walked across the creaking floor and looked closer. The scratches seemed to be haphazard, like a child's scribble. He turned his attention to the world beyond.

To the right, southward and into the sun, the fields rose to a stretch of woodland still bare but faintly tinted with springtime promise: greens and buffs, rosy buds bursting into leaf. The blue sky above, with a flock of drifting clouds grazing across, threw light and shadow over the landscape, timing with the movement of the clouds. Robert stared at the scene, alone in the silent attic.

'What are you up to, Bob? Have you gone to sleep?'

It was his mother's voice that startled him. It rather annoyed him.

'I'm waiting for *you*!' he said. He had stepped quickly back to the open trapdoor. He did not intend to be caught day-dreaming. 'Hand something up. There's plenty of room here!'

Robert, still rather ruffled, stayed at the receiving end of the porterage from below, taking the oddments handed up by his mother and Mrs Green, and stacking them neatly at the further side of the attic. He could do a good job when he wanted to, even when brooding over some imagined grievance no larger than that little scratch on the window in the attic, that lifeless place at the top of the house.

6 ❦ *Nothing Stands Still* ❦

When townspeople go into the country, they have the impression that all is quiet, that nothing ever happens. Even in modern times, with motor traffic roaring on the roads and airplanes across the sky, tourists from town sigh with relief. Many of them even feel uncomfortable, as though what they call the silence means that they have mislaid something. They look at the country folk and either envy them their peaceful lives, or wonder how they can stand the monotony.

If the Bostock family thought either way, they were quickly to be disillusioned.

Mr Bostock telephoned to the castle two days after the arrival at the new home, which Mrs Green said was called Deepdene Farm as long as she had known it, which was all her life, and had been called Deepdene Farm in her great-grandfather's time, these hundreds of years past, because of the woods that lay between its open fields and the grounds of the castle, and being part of the castle estate; the castle, for the reason that the woods went on for miles the other side, being called Deephurst Castle, and that for as long a time as the farm being called Deepdene, both having been built in the distant past, as she was certain of . . .

It was Jennifer who was spellbound by Mrs Green's warm presence, and the confused flow of information about the neighborhood and everything happening in it.

'Tell me, Mrs Green, tell me . . .' her eager inquiries went on all day long. She was as inquisitive as she looked: sharp-featured, quick, and bright-eyed.

But Mr Bostock has been left at the telephone, that second morning at Deepdene Farm. His was the first call after the installation of the line, for nobody had yet rung up from the outside world. New telephones seem always to be shy, after the Exchange has come through to ask if all is working properly.

Mr Bostock rang the castle to ask if he could bring the family to look round. He returned to the lunch table in the dining-room, looking thoughtful.

'Well, dear?' asked his wife.

'The old fellow is very ill, Mary. The son has been sent for. I spoke to a secretary, who said we could go round the gardens if we liked, but . . .'

'Oh, that's callous, John. Is there nothing we can do to help?'

'Well, you know, we are strangers, and everything must be well in hand up there. I imagine the castle is run as efficiently as the works where the money comes from.'

'I didn't see much sign of life when we drove past on our way here.'

'That doesn't signify. The better the machinery, the quieter it is.'

Fortunately, the children had finished their meal and were off on their own affairs during this conversation, which went on from Mrs Bostock's sympathy to her anxiety about the possible effect of the chairman's illness on the huge engineering works, and her husband's new connection with the business.

'Well, nothing ever stands still for long,' said Mr

Bostock, 'and no doubt the old fellow stepped out of it long ago. I've seen him only once, when we started negotiations. Why, that's a year ago. The son who is coming down today will probably take his place. I've found him good to deal with: rather harsh in manner, but knows his job. I suppose he'll take over here if . . .'

But Mr Bostock did not care to forecast gloomy things. He was unlike his son Robert, who at that moment returned to the dining room, and received the news.

'Oh, well, he's very old, isn't he?' And with that remark he dismissed the matter from his mind, at least until next morning, when Mrs Green arrived, with the news that 'the poor old gentleman had gone during the night, but it was a blessing really, he being that helpless, and had been such a proud man, it was terrible to think of him so humbled.'

Michael ignored these words of wisdom. He was interested only in the fact that two sows had arrived at the farm during the morning, along with a man who was to work for Mr Bostock. This was the beginning of the inventor's dream of bringing the long-neglected farm back to prosperity.

Mr Bostock was like so many professional and business men. As soon as they succeed, and make a lot of money, they fulfil a lifelong daydream of going back to the land. They buy a farm, and set out to teach those old-time agriculturalists how to run a farm on scientific and good business lines. The real farmers look on, smile, and say nothing. They just wait.

Mr Bostock was not cocksure, however. For one thing, he had not bought the farm. He was renting it from the great engineering firm with which he was now so prosperously connected. The owners were willing to give him credit, professional advice, and other practical help. He was a brilliant engineer; and modern farming requires a lot of machinery. The part that Nature plays in the undertaking he was willing to learn about from his own future experience and at his own risk, with the help of two or three men of the soil, born into it like oak trees. There are still such countrymen around.

Mr Bostock made a good start with his pig-man, who had a friend known to be first-prize winner three years running at the annual plowing match. This chap wanted to work nearer home. So that was arranged. Then Mrs Green, who could have written an intimate history of Cranehurst and its neighbourhood if she put her mind to it, knew of someone's niece who had gone to a horticultural college and taken a diploma in fruit-growing and general gardening. She, with the help of a laborer, could run the orchard and the garden round the house; the latter job, of course, being shared by the only too eager Mr and Mrs Bostock in their spare time. Mrs Green herself was interested in that also, for she was well named. She assured her employers that she had a green thumb. It is hardly kind merely to call them her employers. By the end of the first week she was one of the family. At least Jennifer, the shrewdest member of the Bostock breed, thought so, and treated her accordingly. Even Michael became attached, though rather more in the manner of a terrier than a human being. That was his character at the age of eight, which may explain why Robert treated him roughly, as he would treat any other dog not prone to instant obedience.

Dogs and small children instinctively fight shy of death. They walk round it when they meet it. They don't even notice it is there. So Michael was off, to introduce himself to the sows, and then to the pig-man.

The sties were away beyond the great barn, spick

and span, ready for the arrival, which had just taken place. Michael stared at the ladies, each in her own apartment, a hut and a yard, brick-built, with a railing round the low brick wall.

The newcomers were still ruffled and indignant, not yet certain if they approved of these quarters. They snuffled and grunted, in and out, testing every corner with their pink snouts.

Michael stood on the wall, clasping the rail, and adoring. He leaned over, stretched out his arm, and touched one scaly back.

'Nay, sonny!' said the pig-man, gently lifting him down. 'That's too risky, man. You get a bite from those jaws and you'd get your hand off! Don't you forget that, now!'

Michael was fearless. Not even Robert had been able to intimidate him. He freed himself from the pig-man's arm, and peered again into the pens, worshiping.

'Why are they so fat?' he asked.

The pig-man laughed.

'Well, you might say that's what they're here for. We hope they'll be giving a good litter in a few weeks' time.'

'Litter?' said the town child. Then he realized, again instinctively, what the word meant. Beatific bliss lit his face, his whole body. He stood rigid with joy.

'Oh!' was all he said, confronted with the prospect of birth.

Down at the farmhouse, the shock of the old chairman's death had made Mrs Green even more than usually informative. Death is a shock even when it is expected, and a welcome release.

She talked of that fact, and explained to Mrs Bostock, who always enjoyed a bit of kindly gossip, how the castle had fallen on evil days, along with the hard times which farmers had at the beginning of the century.

'Must be sixty years ago that the old gentleman's father bought the place. Not much better than a ruin, it was then, like one of those abbeys they used to have hundreds of years ago. But that's history, as you might say. But the family has been rich from the engineering for a long time. His grandfather before him started that up, somewhere in the North, making machines for all sorts: ships and factories and now all these funny-looking affairs for use on the farms. It's mechanics now they want on the fields, not men who know the ways of Nature, and can layer a hedge, and look after the live-stock, as well as the horses.'

From this distinction between the animal life on the farm, which Mrs Bostock noticed with sympathy because she loved riding, Mrs Green returned to the history of the castle, so far as she knew it by word of mouth, and her own life experience. She remembered it as a ruin, when she was a child. The local farmer housed a couple of his workmen, with their families, in part of it. The rest he used as barns and cattle sheds. 'But all that changed when the Old Gentleman and his wife bought the estate.' She never referred to the chairman by name. For her he was the Old Gentleman; she dared approach no nearer. 'His wife was a great Lady, daughter of a duke, but she was that kind and friendly to everybody, especially the people who worked for her. And she had this passion for gardens. All the muck and rubbish was cleared away from around the ruined parts of the castle, and she made a proper paradise, as well as doing up the castle and bringing it to life again. But you'll see for yourself when you go up there, after things have settled down again.'

'Is there no danger of its being sold, now both are dead?'

'Just imagine that! Why, it couldn't happen, after all they've done up there. There's the family to take over. That will mean changes, but things won't come to an end. Of that I'm certain.'

Mrs Green was so certain that she did not find it necessary to explain further. She merely added that one of the sons, who loved the old place, was likely to come and live there, because he was 'a thoughtful gentleman who liked peace and quiet.'

Then she added something that mystified Mrs Bostock, who failed to persuade her to deeper disclosures. 'Mind you, ma'am, there are stories in the village, and have been as long as I remember, that peace and quiet are not what they seem to be, around these old buildings, and even wider afield in these parts!'

7 ❖ *A Visit to the Castle* ❖

The Bostocks, being newcomers, thought it polite to keep out of sight during the next few days, before and after the funeral. Only the Old Gentleman's family attended it, but Mr and Mrs Bostock were invited to a memorial service to be held later in London, where hundreds of friends, and members of the staff of the huge engineering works, would be able to offer their tribute to the famous industrialist.

Robert was shown the invitation.

'Huh!' he said, 'that ought to make you feel safe.'

'From what?' asked his father, passing the card back to Mrs Bostock, and looking at her in sad bewilderment.

'Well, you wouldn't be asked to go if they didn't think of you now as one of the firm.'

'Oh, so that's how you see it?'

Mr Bostock left the room and shut himself in his study.

'What's wrong this time, Mother?' said Bob.

She, too, looked at him; even more sadly than his father had done, but without taking offense.

'I wish I knew, Robert,' she answered. 'But life is rather miserable if we think only about ourselves.'

'I shall have to do just that, starting at a new school,

Mother. If Dad had looked after himself more, you would have had an easier time.'

'I don't know that I should have wanted an easier time, as you call it. But you don't see that yet, do you?'

Mother and son looked at each other, without understanding. Perhaps the sad business up at the castle had settled, like gloomy weather, over the whole estate.

Robert was depressed, and went out. His mother looked through the kitchen window and watched him walking aimlessly up toward the barn, as dark as his own shadow in the sunlight. She saw Michael appear, to wave eagerly to his brother, urging him to come, to hurry. No doubt Michael wanted to show him the pigs, which had been housed for some days and were contentedly settled. Robert, however, had not bothered to make their acquaintance; nor did he do so now. He stopped, shook his head, and turned another way, past the other side of the barn. Both his mother and Michael lost sight of him.

Mrs Bostock now watched Michael. He stood there, in the lee of the barn, a small, disconsolate figure, as if a violent gust of icy wind had struck him. His mother hurried through the scullery, flung open the back door, and waved to him. 'Wait for me. I'm coming!' she cried. 'I want to see the pigs!'

Michael recovered instantly. He ran forward to meet his mother, seized her by the hand, to make her hasten, while he told her that the pig-man had promised him one of the piglets when they were born.

'Won't Jennifer want one?' asked Mrs Bostock.

'Oh, I asked him that, too, and he said yes.'

The distant rebuff from Robert was forgotten. Mrs Bostock tried to share Michael's wild enthusiasm, though she found this to be difficult, in spite of the fact

46

that the sows and their sties were so much cleaner than she had expected.

'Oh, dear, how very maternal they look,' she said.

'What's maternal mean?' asked her son suspiciously.

'Well, I suppose it means motherly,' she had to admit.

That satisfied Michael, and Mrs Bostock left him pouring swill into the two troughs, and receiving the grunts and snorts of the swollen creatures with the utmost rapture.

Mrs Bostock walked slowly back to the house, thinking about Robert, who did not reappear until lunch time, the hour when Mr Bostock came from his study, looking, as usual, exhausted and absentminded, but smiling vaguely. He had been interrupted that morning by Jennifer, who was a great borrower of his books, a strange habit for an eleven-year-old person. It caused frequent requests for an explanation of some passage of prose too difficult even for her sharp wits.

'I was thinking,' said Mr Bostock during the meal, 'now that things are back to normal up at the castle, we might take a look round the gardens, and perhaps . . .'

But at that moment the telephone rang, and he went out to the hall to answer it.

'That's a nice coincidence,' he said as he returned, smiling less vaguely. 'It's the new chief, the son who has been managing director and has been backing my patent all along: same name as his father, John Culverton, a household word in the world of engineering. He has asked us all up to tea.'

'What's his wife like?' said Mrs Bostock instantly.

'His wife? I don't think he's got a wife. No, I'm certain he's a bachelor. He just lives for the firm.'

Mrs Bostock hesitated.

'Won't we be in the way?' she asked, nodding toward Jennifer.

'Is he an ogre?' said that young woman.

'I can hear him crunching your bones,' growled Robert. He glared at Jennifer and gnashed his teeth. That was his idea of a joke.

'You look like you really are!' she said.

Robert instantly changed his tune.

'What do you mean by that?' he demanded angrily.

'Now, no bickering!' said Mrs Bostock. 'But I think you and the boys had better go up without us. We can come another time.'

Her husband would not agree, and the whole family set off at four o'clock for the four-mile drive to the castle. As they approached, after passing over the rising ground, the sunlight across the southern slope changed the new string in the hop garden to burnished gold, long, diminishing avenues of geometrical glory between the poles.

'My word! Look at that!' cried Mr Bostock, taking one hand from the steering.wheel, to point at the miracle made every springtime with the stringing in the hop gardens of Kent.

'Careful, John!' cried Mrs Bostock, as the car thumped over a small pothole, one of many made by the outbreak of miniature water springs forever bursting through the tarmac surface of the lane.

But the children ignored both interruptions. They were interested only in the tall tower with its two hex-agonal wings crowned by weather vanes. The sun shone beyond the tower, so that it stood in shadow, its ancient rose-red brickwork temporarily dark and ominous. It loomed over the landscape.

As the car approached, the lower stretches of the

castle appeared, at right angles to the tower, drenched in light and warmth. Formal gardens surrounded the buildings, and Mr Bostock drew up at a break in the tall yew hedge.

The family trod the flagstone path shyly to the front door, which was like that of the farmhouse, but larger and with even more ironwork.

An old manservant opened the door. He was not very smart. He wore a dusty waistcoat with sleeves. His trousers were baggy.

'That's not a proper footman,' whispered Jennifer to her mother, who hushed her. But the old man had heard, and he eyed the small girl with wicked glee. She saw the glance, and sheltered behind her mother as the man opened the door wider and grudgingly invited the visitors to enter.

This rather hostile reception, however, was instantly changed to a real welcome. The new master of the house appeared from a passage at the back of the hall.

'Ha, my dear Bostock! So this is your family! Good to see you all. We need some young life, after recent events. Nice to think of you as our neighbors, eh? How appropriate, to come with springtime! I hope you approve of the farmhouse, Mrs Bostock?'

While Mr Culverton was speaking, Robert was aware of being inspected with special attention. For once, he felt no suspicion of a stranger. Mr Culverton was tall and strongly built, with a powerful head. He was pleasant and smiling now, but behind this good humor lay something that made Mrs Bostock and Jennifer draw together again.

However, Mr Culverton was a courteous host. He invited Mrs Bostock to sit at the head of the long table in front of the enormous open fireplace. It occupied one whole side of the room into which he had ushered his visitors. A woman entered, carrying a tray with the tea-pot under a cozy, the milk jug, sugar bowl, and a plate piled high with buttered crumpets. After a quick glance at Mr Culverton, who nodded, she set the tray before Mrs Bostock. The host sat down between Jennifer and Michael, opposite Robert, so Mr Bostock had to take the vacant chair at the other end of the table.

Nothing had been said, but this placing of the tea party, and the assumption that Mrs Bostock should pre-side, instantly removed all shyness. Conversation began to flow, and the crumpets to circulate, while Mrs Bos-tock poured the tea.

Mr Culverton asked the children if they had ex-plored the farm, the management of which was now being handed over to their father.

'We are precisionists, eh, Bostock? What do you say to that? You have no fears on that score, Mrs Bostock: your husband running two jobs together? He is hand-picking his workers. My father had no interest in agriculture, apart from making tools for it. Unsatis-factory, really! I want our practice here to improve that side of the engineering. We shall better adapt the tool to the job.'

He looked across the table to Robert.

'But forgive me, I'm talking shop! Are you interested in these matters, young man?'

The 'young man' was more interested in the crum-pets, and in the other eatables which had already been set on the table when the guests entered the room. Robert was red in the face, but that may have been caused by the fire of huge logs flickering lazily on the pile of wood ash accumulated during the winter. Though the April day was warm and sunny, the interior of the castle, like that of the farmhouse, was cavernous, and permanently chilly.

Robert, leaning over his plate, looked up. He was aware of something powerful. It was strange to him. He knew only his father's kindly, evasive eyes, and his mother's gentle ones inclined to sadness when in repose.

He was attracted. He was commanded. It was a challenge. He felt that for once he was treading on firm ground, of his own choosing.

'Yes, I am,' he said. Then he added, as an afterthought, 'sir!'

Mr Culverton studied him with increased interest, then switched off the power, and turned his more easy attention to the rest of the family.

After tea he took them round the castle, which his grandfather and father had restored. He did not say much about the treasures that enriched it, except when Mrs Bostock or Jennifer inquired about some particular object: a fourposter bed, a lovely cabinet, a period-piece chair, a Persian rug, a picture, or a vase. Jennifer kept him busy over these details, but he answered with patience and amusement.

'I can foresee her future,' he whispered, drawing Mrs Bostock aside. 'She will be the first woman Keeper of the British Museum. Those shrewd eyes miss nothing. And so knowledgeable, too!'

Robert overheard this, and he wandered away, into the next room, already explored.

'Come along, Bob,' called his mother, her attention divided into pleasure at Mr Culverton's praise of Jennifer and anxiety at Robert's disgust for it.

'Boys hardly notice such things,' she said to her host.

'No,' he said. 'I've lived with these treasures all my life, but it took me a long time to realize what they are worth.'

51

'Worth?' said Robert, who had rejoined the party. 'They must be worth millions!'

'Oh, Robert, no!' cried his mother. But Mr Culverton laughed, clapped Robert on the shoulder, and hustled him along to find Mr Bostock and Michael, who had moved on and disappeared, the father unwilling to leave the Tyke unattended, for fear of breakages.

'There are all kinds of values, my boy,' said Mr Culverton. 'You'll find that out later, especially by living down here, in this ancient estate. Something gets hold of one, you know. Why, you must already have heard that we have a ghost, and visitations out of the past? That's part of our capital value too. Can you put a price on that, as well as these pictures and tapestries and antiques?'

'I don't believe in all that,' said Robert; and he was really sulky, in spite of Mr Culverton's powerful personality.

'Well, believe it or not, the legend persists. You see, Robert—does this interest you, Mrs Bostock?—during the eighteenth century, when England was constantly at war with France, a party of French naval officers was interned here. I think it was around 1760, long before the French Revolution and the rise of Napoleon. The story is that they had a pretty good time; even kept their own horses and had local races in the park here, now part of the home farm. In those days wars were run with rules, at least amongst the officers of the opposing sides: dueling on a grand scale. If you were a prisoner and on parole, you kept your word. Even away back in the Middle Ages a king of France was captured and spent over twenty years in England, on parole. He spent his time writing poetry. You can find out about that from your history books.'

Robert scowled. He felt that he was being bullied; that somebody stronger willed than himself was on the attack. It was a novelty, not known in the family, for even the shrewd and artful Jennifer rarely operated against him. So he was puzzled. He did not know how to take this.

'History!' he muttered, as scornfully as he dared.

'Yes, real enough at the time,' said Mr Culverton. 'Make no mistake about that, young man. What happened in the past makes us what we are today, wouldn't you agree?'

Robert was still suspicious and resentful, so he did not reply. But Mr Culverton ignored that and went on with his story, the history of the castle, while steering Mrs Bostock, Jennifer (who was spellbound) and Robert through two more salons to the farther and minor staircase at the west end of the castle block, the magnificent remains of the sixteenth-century four-sided building, similar to an Oxford college.

Mr Bostock and Michael must have gone down this staircase and out to the open air. Through the long window, they could be seen in the garden below, the child tugging at his father's hand, impatient to be somewhere else than where he was, which is the way with infants and butterflies.

8 ❋ *The Writing on the Window* ❋

Easter came a week later. By then Jennifer and Michael had explored the castle garden and the nearer acres of the farm, down to the little river that flowed through the middle of it, after feeding the moat and the two lakes, one of which was filled with reeds and bulrush, matted with layers of dead stuff, driftage of many autumns. Waterfowl nested there, noisy and invisible until disturbed by some danger from dry ground: a fox, a dog, a human with a gun. At that alarm, the reeds quivered, parted, and wild wings beat up; honkings and shrieks betrayed the fugitives rushing suicidally to the open water of the lower lake, or taking to equally exposed flight.

The two children were not happy down there. That treacherous mat of rubbish closed around the reeds had been tested by their shoe tips. It swayed at the touch, and a clunking sound of water came from beneath it.

'That's like quicksand,' said the cautious Jennifer, snatching Michael back. 'Let's go away.'

Michael was willing, for there was much more to see around the farm and countryside. Everything was new to him: the plowed fields, the hedgerows with springtime flowers; above all, the sties behind the great barn.

Wherever Jennifer led him, he contrived to work his way back to those two sows, content to watch and wait.

'It's only going to be natural,' said Jennifer, half

afraid of her young brother's eagerness. But her wisdom was meaningless to him, and he ignored it. The kind pig-man had given him a promise. That was good enough for Michael. Though the family called him the Tyke because he darted about like a fox terrier, he had a passion for living creatures, furred or feathered. That may be why Jennifer drew him away from that dangerous submerged lake, with its enticing colony of coots, moorhens, and wild duck.

Robert was not interested in Michael's safety. He went off each day; a lone wolf. He told nobody where he had been or what he had done. He came back at mealtimes, his pockets bulging.

Good Friday was hot and sunny. Robert took off his tweed coat before sitting down to lunch. It collapsed on a chair like a sack of coal.

'Whatever have you got in those pockets?' said his mother, lifting the coat and draping it over the chair back. 'It weighs a ton!'

She took a couple of fine round pebbles from one pocket.

'Why, Bob!' said his father. 'Are you studying geology?'

'It's ammunition,' was Robert's reply.

'Ammunition? Whatever for?'

'You never know,' he muttered.

There was silence round the table. Heads were lowered over soup plates, but Robert saw Jennifer's wicked glance at her mother. That is how he took it.

'Anything wrong with defending yourself?' he demanded.

'Why, who's to attack you in this peaceful spot?' said Mr Bostock. 'What's biting you, my boy?'

'I've been looking around,' Robert replied. 'I went into Cranehurst to see what the school looked like. An easy bike ride: but I saw some really tough characters standing about the High Street; the sort that gang up; rougher even than the town types in London.'

'What a warlike world you live in, Bob,' said his father. 'I'm sorry for you.'

'You need not be sorry for me. I can look after myself! I know my way about.'

'You're like Jack the Giant Killer,' said Jennifer.

Everybody laughed, and even Robert relaxed. 'You've got a name for everything, smartie,' he said, but not too unkindly.

'She hasn't named our ghost yet,' said Mr Bostock. 'You'd better get busy on that, Jenny. He might take offense.'

'He or she?' asked Mrs Bostock, setting a great dish of grilled Dover sole before her husband, while Jennifer collected the empty soup plates. Potatoes and spring greens were brought from the stove, and the Bostocks set to work on the second course: no fasting on their Good Friday, for they were not a deeply religious family, though the mother had been to Cranehurst Church on the first Sunday in the new home, to hear an eloquent sermon and to be greeted after the service by a rubicund and friendly vicar.

That was why the Bostocks were eating fish on Good Friday. The novelty of this switched the conversation from Bob's warlike interests.

'You seem to have toured the neighborhood, Bob. What about giving me a hand to hoist that crate up into the attics? I've cleared the books out of it. Let's do it this afternoon!'

'I've not been up there!' cried Jennifer. 'May I help, too?'

Michael did not volunteer. He was afraid interesting events might begin in the pigsties when he was up under the roof of the farmhouse, much too far from the scene of action.

'My dear!' said Mr Bostock to his wife—rather breathlessly because he and Robert were pausing half-way up the stairs, the cumbersome crate between them, with Mrs Bostock and Jennifer anxiously following to protect the balusters, the stair carpets, and the furniture on the landings.

Mr Bostock recovered his breath. 'My dear, how remarkable! Only a week have we been here, and the house has changed: a subtle change! It has become a home, *our* home. You know, it is really quite mysterious. How is it done?'

'I cannot imagine, John!' she replied dryly. 'But Mrs Green—no, I mean Kate, and I have each lost pounds in weight.'

'Wonderful! Wonderful, Mary. Now, Bob, back to more tangible jobs! Are you ready? Then up!'

The procession staggered round the bend to the last landing and halted by the little alcove. Robert hooked the pole into the ring on the trapdoor, and swung down the ladder.

The family stood, surveying the aperture and the crate.

'Had it occurred to you to measure them first?' asked Mrs Bostock sweetly.

'Oh, good heavens!' exclaimed the great scientific inventor, now to become famous throughout the whole world of engineering. 'Robert, why didn't you think of that? You're a man of action, aren't you?'

Robert meanwhile used the pole as a measuring rod, first against the crate, then against the base of the aluminum steps.

'Well,' he said, 'it will go up the steps, with an inch

57

to spare; so it will go through the trapdoor, which is wider still.'

'Marvelous!' said his father, with an expression of reverence on his face, adding to its habitual kindliness. 'You've saved our skin, boy!'

'We shall probably lose some, getting the brute up through that hole.'

Bob was not being sarcastic. He was pleased by his father's praise, and amused by his innocence.

'Let me go first, please!' cried Jennifer. 'I've not been up there yet.' Like a squirrel, she cleared the steps in a couple of seconds, and ran across the attic to enjoy the view from the dormer window.

When the rest of the party, with the crate, appeared, she was seen crouching on the wide window-seat, naming aloud the features of the landscape as she recognized them: the wavering line of willows and alders along the river, the various fields whose names she had already memorized, the woods up the slope, and the top of the castle tower rising out of them, above the ridge that hid the building and the gardens round it.

Mrs Bostock sat on the crate, watching Jennifer. She was secretly proud of this observant, quick-witted daughter. She was also careful never to speak about this cleverness in front of Robert, the firstborn, who so frequently puzzled her.

Jennifer suddenly noticed the scratched pane of glass in the leaded window. She frowned as she studied it, and wiped it a little cleaner with her hand. 'Look, Daddy!' she exclaimed. 'It's writing!'

She examined it more closely.

'Why, it's a name! What a long one! I can see it now. It must be a foreign one.'

She spelled it out slowly, letter by letter.

'Raymond de Crétien.'

She went over it again, with more emphasis. 'Why, it's a French name! It must be one of those prisoners Mr Culverton told us about!'

'It can't be,' said her mother. 'What would he be doing here, four miles away. That would have been out of bounds, surely?'

'A nice point,' said Mr Bostock. 'What do you think of Jennifer's powers of detection, Bob?'

He looked round; but Robert was not there. His momentary good humor after his father's praise had been instantly shattered by Jennifer's clever discovery that what he had dismissed as mere scratches on the glass were the letters of a name.

He was so angry with himself, and therefore with Jennifer, that he slipped silently down the steps and back to his room.

'What's wrong now?' asked Mr Bostock.

'Oh, one of his moods,' said Jennifer.

'Don't you be so sharp; you'll cut yourself one of these days.'

The reprimand came from her mother, who always covered up for Robert on such occasions. Though she could not understand what Jennifer called 'his moods', she believed there was something worth-while in him, struggling to get out. Most mothers are like that.

The three Bostocks examined the signature closely.

'It must have been done with a diamond,' said Jennifer.

'Where would he have got that?' said her mother.

'That's simple enough,' said Mr Bostock. 'That name suggests a nobleman, and he would be wearing a diamond ring. A likely explanation, eh?'

He studied the scratchings again.

'Look at the curlicues and scrolls! Like those initial letters in medieval manuscript books. I'm not surprised

Bob missed the writing. He may have thought it was a spider's web.'

'Bob wouldn't be interested,' said Jennifer wistfully. 'He doesn't believe in history.'

'Oh, is that so? Did he say that?'

'Not really: but if I talk about things like that, he laughs or slaps me down. It depends on his moods.'

'That's enough,' said Mrs Bostock. 'We can't all have the same interests.'

'What *does* interest him?' demanded Jennifer defiantly.

'I wish we knew.' Mr Bostock spoke rather sadly. 'We'd all get along better with him then.'

'Oh, leave the boy alone,' cried his wife. She was so upset that she climbed down the steps and left father and daughter together.

'But a man wouldn't wear a diamond ring?' mused Jennifer.

'Oh, yes; in those days, before the French Revolution, the aristocrats were as showy as the newly rich. They refused to see what was coming to them. They paraded their wealth. That was partly the cause of the trouble.'

'I see,' said Jennifer. 'Yes, I read about that in *A Tale of Two Cities.*'

Her father chuckled.

'I bet you've beaten Bob there!'

'Oh, he's read it, too. He told me about the guillotine. That was the part he liked best.'

'Is that so?' Mr Bostock spoke thoughtfully. Then he changed the subject.

'Well, well! We'd better go down. It's dusty and stuffy up here. But that poor fellow must have spent a long time here. I suppose he had to amuse himself somehow. Was he locked in, I wonder?'

9 ✤ *The Tale of the French Lieutenant* ✤

Not everybody was critical of Robert. Mr Culverton up at the castle took a liking to him at first sight. He telephoned, the day after the tea party, to speak to Mr Bostock about some business matter connected with the patent rights on a further development of the invention, which was adding to the wealth of the firm and making a nice fortune for Mr Bostock.

'Tell that lad of yours that he's welcome to explore the library here,' he concluded. 'I think he's worth encouraging.'

'I'm glad to hear you say so.'

'You sound doubtful, Bostock.'

'Not at all! Not at all! But you know, Culverton—fathers and sons, and all that. An awkward relationship, especially with a boy of that age.'

He heard Mr Culverton laugh over the telephone. 'You mean the old stag and the young stag! The clash of antlers, eh, Bostock? Well, let him rage a little. Do him good to browse in this library. He might find what he isn't looking for. That sort of thing can happen, you know. We're all liable to stumble over something we didn't know was in our path, and it proves to be just what we need.'

Mr Bostock told his wife, and they discussed the invitation. She was uneasy about it.

'What's wrong, Mary?'

'Isn't Mr Culverton rather fierce? You know how sulky Robert can be. He may say something—'

'He's more likely to refuse to say something if Culverton drives him too hard or too fast. But Bob will get as good as he gives, and that's what the boy wants. We're too close to him. We can't do it. It will come naturally from Culverton. He's made that way. He's powerful and will ride Bob down if necessary.'

Mrs Bostock looked at her husband reproachfully.

'Bob's the only person in this world that you're not gentle with.'

She said no more. Later in the day, however, she told Robert of the invitation, and to her surprise he responded with enthusiasm.

'Can we go, too?' cried Jennifer, who had the habit of overhearing other people's conversation. Her ears were as lively as her eyes.

'Not until you're invited, Jenny. And Michael is too young to be interested in a library like that; all those folio volumes and first editions.'

Michael did not hear that. He was out, amongst the farm buildings, near those pigsties.

A few days later, Robert decided to go up to the castle. He had been thinking about that signature on the window in the attic. The annoyance that Jennifer had found what he had overlooked was forgotten. Annoyance was replaced by curiosity, a faculty the family had not observed in him; not even Jennifer.

The villainous old retainer, wearing the waistcoat with sleeves, leered at Robert suspiciously when the boy presented himself at the castle. The great door stood open, for the April day was fine and warm. But as Robert entered the hall, he left the warmth outside. It came no farther than the slab of sunshine that lay athwart the first few flagstones of the hall floor.

62

'You been asked up?' demanded the old man.

Robert did not have to reply, for Mr Culverton appeared.

'Ah, Robert, so you've come to look round our shelves? A mixed bag, you know. My father and grand-father both collected. You won't find a lot of technical stuff, if that's what you fancy. Are you engineering-minded, like your father?'

Robert denied this emphatically, after greeting his host politely enough, but without overdoing it.

'Well, what *does* interest you, Robert? You're an outdoor man, I fancy. Travel books, wildlife, eh, is that your line of country?'

Even had Robert known how to reply, he would have found no opportunity, for Mr Culverton was so friendly and talkative. He showed no sign of that hard-ness and fierceness which had frightened Mrs Bostock. And he treated Robert as man to man. That made Robert find his tongue also, and to his own surprise he began to respond to the flood of information flowing from his host.

'Can you tell me about this story of a ghost haunt-ing the castle?' he asked. He was not sure why he said that, but something at the back of his mind, lurking there since the matter was first mentioned by his father, suddenly made Robert inquire about it.

He and Mr Culverton were in the library, a very long, narrow chamber, with a dais at one end on which stood a grand pianoforte. The mullioned windows were the only breaks in the book-lined walls; rows and rows of shelves, with books of all sizes, from folio to duo-decimo, most of them bound in leather, powdered and roughened with age, like autumn leaves on the winter floor of the woodlands.

Robert's question, coming so abruptly into the conversation, made Mr Culverton stop talking. He stared thoughtfully at the piano, and Robert saw his face harden.

'Music!' said Mr Culverton. Robert was puzzled, almost frightened.

'That's another world, my boy. You can't grasp it, you can't grasp it! What music means to me, I suppose these stories about ghosts and other worlds mean to these people who believe in such things. All beyond our understanding, Robert! That's what it is, believe me! We can't deny it, any more than we can deny what music does to us. It leads us on, I tell you. It leads us on! It's not a matter of quality. It's a matter of power. A drumbeat can do it, or a bell tolling. So it is with these superstitions. We educate ourselves out of them. Science dismisses them. But they come back; they come back!'

He was struggling with something invisible to Robert; invisible to himself. But after a moment or two, he conquered it, and the hardness disappeared. He was friendly again.

'I'll tell you the story,' he said, and took one of the smaller books from a shelf near the huge open fireplace, where three sawn sections of tree trunk rested in a pile of wood ash that smelled of the centuries, perfuming the whole of the library with the scent of the past, though the fire was not alight.

'Here it is. Sit you down, my boy, and I'll give you the gist of the long story. I won't bore you with the whole of it.'

The library door to the garden faced east, and no sunlight, except a quickly narrowing slant, penetrated at midmorning. Robert, perched on a wooden bench by a long table, felt his body shrinking as he grew more and more chilly while Mr Culverton picked his way through the narrative, choosing passages to read aloud.

Robert was suspicious again, and he did not enjoy

64

the cold creeping over him. He wanted to cry out that he did not believe all this nonsense about the persistence of the dead. But Mr Culverton was not a person who could be stopped or contradicted. He was too powerful. When he looked up from the book to further the story through his own words, his eyes glittered like two splinters of quartz in a mass of sullen rock. Robert listened, spellbound, in spite of his unwillingness to believe. 'Don't tell me that stuff,' he wanted to say. But he didn't say it. He could not. His blood was flowing too slowly in his veins.

'You see,' said Mr Culverton, 'there must be something in this legend which has persisted for two hundred years. It was 1760 when England was at war with France. French naval officers captured in battle were housed in the castle here. We can't say they were imprisoned, for in those days there was a code of honor among the nobility throughout Europe, a relic of the days of medieval chivalry. It set them apart from the rest of the population of their countries. There were class distinctions then, especially in France. It wasn't easy to make silk purses out of sows' ears in those days. But the people of France found a way to do it during the Revolution, which followed less than thirty years after 1760, the year of our story.

'All those French naval officers living here were aristocrats, and were treated as such. Being on parole, they were free to do as they liked, but within the bounds fixed by our authorities at that time. It was all much more personal than the rules during our last two wars. There were fewer people concerned, and that makes a vast difference.'

Robert was getting bored by these dry slices of history, but Mr Culverton now said something that alarmed him, which brought him to life again.

'But it's lunch time, Robert, and I've still not told you the story of the French lieutenant. Look! I'll ring up the farmhouse and tell them you're eating here. We can talk during the meal.'

Robert tried to protest. He felt shy and clumsy. But, as his father had predicted, Mr Culverton 'rode him down' by leading the way to a small room, half study, half office, which lay beyond the great dining hall adjoining the library.

'Cozy enough here, Robert?' said Mr Culverton, throwing a couple of logs on the small fire. The warmth encouraged Robert, and so did the simple meal of cold roast beef with potatoes cooked in their jackets.

'A glass of red wine won't hurt you, man,' said Mr Culverton, pouring claret from a decanter into two glasses. No servant appeared. The potatoes were taken from a covered dish standing on an electric hot plate on a side table.

'We use that vast place only on state occasions,' said Mr Culverton pointing with his knife toward the dining hall through which he had conducted Robert to the study.

'I'm more frequently alone here now, and likely to be, now both my parents have gone. They kept open house. Not so easy for a bachelor, especially nowadays in a house like this, without an army of servants.'

Robert was not really comfortable, for he was in a world strange to him; everything on a big scale, yet informal and oddly quiet. He ate his beef and potatoes guardedly, not caring to look around, or to return the open interest with which he sensed that Mr Culverton was studying him. The grim friendliness would not let him retire into himself. It broke through that secretive habit.

'Does the young wine suit you?'

Robert was obliged to taste it. He found the flavor indefinite, something he had never known before. It lingered on his tongue. He sipped again, and looked up to see Mr Culverton watching him closely. He had to say something. 'It's interesting.'

His host was amused. The heavy features broke into a smile of approval.

'Good! You show promise, my boy. When you make your way in the world, as you should do, you'll become more acquainted with good wine. But now let us go on with our story. I can do without the book. That young lieutenant has been one of the household since long before my family took over.'

They sat facing each other across the table as Mr Culverton continued the tale.

'I've explained to you what parole meant among officers in those days, whatever their nationality. It was a matter of honor. Now nobody knows exactly what caused this young French gentleman to break parole, and thus get himself into trouble with his fellow prisoners. Being pent up here, they found life tedious, no doubt, though they were allowed to have their horses, which they rode badly, being sailors. They used to race between the stables and the top of the rise where the drive from the public road cuts through the copse, once part of the great wood of oaks and beech.

'But I fancy this young fellow was odd man out. Somebody went through the papers left behind after the prisoners were released when a temporary peace was signed. There were letters, diaries, all manner of stuff which King George III's Government confiscated, looking for information likely to be useful should war break out again between England and France.

'It seems that this fellow was unpopular. Some thought him a prig. A few of the real swells, ducal family men with long pedigrees, recorded that there was something rotten in his family tree. You understand me?'

Robert was not sure, but he appreciated the idea. He nodded approvingly, but did not reply, for Mr Culverton had resumed his story.

'This chap didn't ride. He kept to himself and took no part in the rough play with which his comrades broke the monotony. Incidentally, they also, bit by bit, broke up the castle, for when they left the place was half ruined. Time and neglect did the rest. We've got records of that, too, and a few paintings which I must show you one day: romantic, but sordid in fact.

'It appears that in one of these roughhouse bouts, this Lieutenant Raymond de Crétien—'

'What did you say?' cried Robert. 'What name was that?'

Mr Culverton looked at him in surprise, and some annoyance at the shrill interruption.

'Raymond de Crétien,' he repeated, slowly articulating each syllable. 'So he would have been one of some noble family, probably provincial nobility, pretty rustic in their manners.'

'But sir!' said Robert, now thoroughly excited, 'that is the name scratched on the windowpane in the attic!'

'Which attic?'

'In the farmhouse! We found it last week when we were stowing stuff away up there.'

Mr Culverton rose from his chair, then sat down again.

'Well, that's clever of you, my boy! You've found a clue to the mystery. It connects up with the legend. By God, that's well done!'

He beamed on Robert. The boy was so warmed by this sudden outbreak of praise that he did not care to say that his young sister, Jennifer, and not himself, had deciphered the scratches.

'Take some cheese,' said Mr Culverton. And this command prevented Robert from correcting the mistake.

'Yes, it explains a lot. The story is that this fellow became so miserable at the way he was treated by his fellow officers—they may have sent him to Coventry, or even beaten him up—that his nerve went and with it, his morale. At any rate, he broke parole. He disappeared, and for a couple of weeks there was not a sign of him. During that time the fellow countrymen, whom he deserted, were confined to barracks, as you might say. It was foolish and unfair, but that's what happens in wartime. A great many stupid people get a brief authority. Those poor devils were not allowed outside the castle walls. What's more, they felt the disgrace. A French gentleman and officer had broken his word. He had probably got away to France. They vowed that after the war, when they, too, returned, he would be called to account. The code of conduct was strict in those days.

'In fact, he didn't get back to France. Two weeks later, he was fool enough, or gentleman enough, to come back to the castle. Nobody knew what happened, or where he had been, until you youngsters found that signature. I must ask your father to let me see it. Rumor says that, at the time, one of the women who came in daily to cook and clean took a fancy to this melancholy misfit. Maybe she lived in the farmhouse; one of the tenant's daughters, perhaps. She may have sheltered him there. Who knows? A likely thing, Robert. Women have small regard for rules and regulations.'

Robert yawned and longed to escape.

'But wait a minute.' Mr Culverton was amused.

69

Nothing went unnoticed by him. 'Before the officer of the guard could intervene, Count Raymond de Crétien disappeared again. He had come back after dark, and the first people who saw him were his own countrymen. They, too, disobeyed orders. They broke out of confinement to barracks, which was only a formal matter, took the poor chap down to the lake, strangled him, tied something heavy to his body, and flung it into the upper lake, which probably in those days was clear and part of the lower one, before the stream was diverted to prevent the moat from overflowing.'

Robert was interested again.

'Can't we search for the body, sir?'

'What? After two hundred years?'

Mr Culverton may have been joking, but he spoke deliberately, even solemnly, as he added, 'Besides, the poor young man isn't there! He's wandering about the estate looking for something. The legend is that he wants a decent burial, on his family estate in France.'

Mr Culverton so impressed young Bostock that the boy lost all sense of reality. He saw his host as something other than human; a figure hewn out of granite.

'What d'you think of that?' said the statue.

Bob frowned. He was struggling against himself, as well as against this intimidatory person who had entertained him to luncheon.

'I don't believe that last bit,' he said; and he spoke with force, angrily, rudely.

That broke the spell. Mr Culverton rose from the table.

'Well, my boy, you seem to know your own mind. That's a good thing if you happen to be right.'

Then Mr Culverton dismissed him, with the reminder that he was welcome to come and read in the library at any time.

'Old Collins will let you in,' he said, as Robert followed him to the door of that noble room. Old Collins was the resident caretaker, the last of a staff of retainers. He was the hostile character in the waistcoat with sleeves.

'Not likely,' thought Robert, as he recalled that leering visage and the rheumatic limp. The boy quickened his pace as he began the four-mile walk along the lane to the farmhouse. After the castle was out of sight, he slowed down under the weight of thought. He looked over the parkland to his right and saw the sky reflected in the open water of the lower lake. April clouds passed over it and a flight of duck. The upper lake, like a blind eye, lay in front of the woodland beyond. It kept its secret.

Robert stared at it, frowned, then stolidly moved on. But before he lost sight of the lakes, as the lane curved away to the left, he stopped, and half against his will, looked over the hedge. Sunlight and shadow moved over the meadows pronouncing the bright April green, then reducing it again. That upper lake, a rusty old carpet of dead rushes, merely changed from dusk to dark.

Robert studied it for some minutes, frowned, shook his head obstinately, then walked on.

When a family suddenly becomes prosperous, its daily life can be enlarged and lightened. It was so with the Bostocks, especially Mrs Bostock, who loved the country and had longed for a garden all her married life, which had been spent in a suburban London villa, dingy and out of date. Now she had the spacious farmhouse, a walled garden, lawns, flower beds, and shrubberies; beyond that, the farm and its complex of outbuildings, all set in the generous landscape of park, woodlands, and distant hills, the great chalk Downs.

Mr Bostock, always a happy man because of his inventive genius as an engineer, now also had the running of the farm as an additional delight. He longed for a thirty-six-hour day. Though that was impossible, he managed to fit in with family life. Not that his wife nor Jennifer and Michael complained of being neglected.

The two children, indeed, had no time to feel neglected. When summer term started after the Easter holidays, their mother drove them to the school at Cranehurst every morning and fetched them at three thirty. The rest of the day was theirs. Both had new bicycles to ride around the private lanes and paths on the estate and the farm. What more could a girl of eleven and a boy aged eight want? They lived in a paradise of their own, rich in fur and feather, and other wonders and surprises of nature.

Robert was provided with a bicycle more for use than for pleasure. He, too, began the summer term, but at Cranehurst Grammar School, and had to ride to and from the little town as a day boy. He did not get home until around five o'clock in the evening, often later.

He said nothing about the grim adventure of starting life at a new school. Jennifer and Michael were talkative enough about their junior school. Both immediately found friends, who were brought in twos and threes to the farm, and had to be taken home later by poor Mrs Bostock, or fetched by parents who must be entertained to drinks with conversation. Within a few weeks the neighborliness had spread widely around the countryside, centered upon these two perpetually excited and enraptured children.

'Well, Bob,' said Mr Bostock to Robert, one evening at the end of April. The family were seated at dinner, an early meal because Mrs Bostock was strict about the younger children not going late to bed. 'We've not heard anything about your new school. What d'you think of it? Fitting in all right? Met any people you like, masters or boys?'

There was an uneasy silence. Father looked at mother. Jennifer's keen glance flashed round the family, from face to face. Even Michael paused from stuffing himself in his eagerness to get away to something or other he had in hand out of doors.

'Well, anything wrong there?' persisted Mr Bostock, ignoring his wife's silent signal for caution.

Robert writhed under the torment, for that was how his father's inquiry affected him. He leaned over his plate, took another forkful of food and growled, 'Foul!'

'Oh, Robert, so soon?' pleaded his mother.

73

'Soon enough to try their tricks on me,' he said, growing angry in recollection.

'Did they begin on you straightaway, Bob?' asked his father more kindly, no longer teasing him.

'Not exactly. But they wanted to know too much. They knew I came from London, like some of the boarders. And that's a gang-up you see. But because I'm a day boy, I'm not wanted there and the locals don't want me either.'

Nobody knew what to say, while Robert brooded over his troubles.

'Look here!' he said, and he put down his knife and fork, for he was trembling with rage. 'You know why I was late home the other night? I'll tell you. I found my tires flat and my pump stolen!'

'Not *stolen*?' said Mrs Bostock.

'Well, it looked like that. It was gone anyway. I had to search round the bicycle shed and couldn't find it. So I helped myself to another fellow's pump; one of the boarders. All the day boys were gone by then. And that led to a row.'

'Why, surely the boy didn't mind your using his pump?'

'Not at first, but there were other chaps in the shed, and I let them know what I thought of the dirty trick. One of them reached up and took my pump from a beam where it had been hidden. I asked him if he'd done that, and he wouldn't say yes or no. It turns out he was a prefect.'

'Was there a fight?' It was Michael's angelic voice.

Usually Robert ignored questions from that quarter, but now he was so bewitched that he had lost contact with his surroundings. The family, the dining-room in his house, were gone. He was back in that school bicycle shed some days ago.

74

'I was ready for one, I'll tell you! But that chap clipped the pump onto my bike and walked off. The others followed him without a word. I might have been a leper!'

'Did you go white?' said Jennifer. 'Lepers go snow white.'

Robert glared at her. 'Is that meant to be funny?' he said.

Nobody replied. Robert hesitated, then left the table and the dining room. The old staircase creaked under his tread, and his mother winced at the sound.

'Thank goodness tomorrow is Sunday,' she said. 'He'll have a day to cool down. But why do you provoke him so—you and Father?'

She was more worried than cross with Jennifer, whose quick jibes were never charged with malice. But Robert could not realize that.

What made the situation more delicate was that next day was not only Sunday; it was also Robert's birthday.

Every family has its special ceremony for these occasions. The Bostocks' method was to keep silent about a birthday until the very morning. Everybody assembled at the breakfast table; still not a word said. But piled on the plate at the lucky member's place at the table were the gifts, in their wrappings, with notes attached.

Even Robert had to acknowledge that life has its bright moments, when he appeared, rather gummy-eyed after his outburst on the Saturday evening, which had left the whole family disturbed until night and sleep closed all eyes.

He looked round at the four faces and smiled sheepishly. 'Jolly good of you,' he said.

'Go on, go on, open them,' urged Michael.

Robert was about to do so. Indeed, the first parcel was half unwrapped when there was a knock at the scullery door and the pig-man appeared at the open door of the dining room.

'Beg pardon,' he said, 'but one lot has come! All ten of them! And she's taking them that tenderly. A pretty sight it is, not one overlaid!'

Michael was gone, vanished like a trout under a sunbeam. He was followed by Jennifer. Robert's birthday ceremony and the opening of his presents were thrust into the background.

Mr Bostock hesitated, then rose and patted Robert on the shoulder. 'Sorry, my boy. But I'd better go and see that everything is in hand there.' And he was gone, too.

Robert and his mother sat alone at the breakfast-table. She saw the light die from his eyes.

'Will you wait for them to come back, Bob?' she whispered.

'Why?' he said, 'they don't much care, do they?'

'That's not fair, darling.'

Mrs Bostock was almost in tears as she watched Robert tear the three parcels open, and put the contents down without a word of comment. Why bother about Jennifer's and Michael's gifts? They were not there to see the effect. Mrs Bostock's was the largest parcel. It contained a suede leather coat. Robert stared at it, incredulous. He flushed and, at last, looked up at his mother.

'That's jolly nice,' he said. 'You knew what I wanted, Mother.'

'That's what mothers are for, Bob,' she replied, almost with relief. 'Better see if it fits.'

It did. Robert sat down again, still wearing it.

'There's one more,' said Mrs Bostock.

Bob took up the envelope which had been hidden by the parcels. It was his father's gift. He opened it, and found three pound notes, and a card on which Mr Bostock must have written overnight.

Dear Bob,
Put this toward something you really want, and forgive those that you think have trespassed against you.

Robert read the note, put the money in a pocket of his new leather coat, then looked at his mother. 'And it ends up with a sermon,' he said bitterly. 'I suppose he's now gone to preach to the pigs on *their* birthday. That makes eleven of us!'

Mrs Bostock was about to say something, but stopped herself with a little gesture of dismay, as though a wasp were hovering before her face. She rose, and began to clear the breakfast table. Still Robert sat brooding.

'Will you give me a hand?' said his mother. 'A little help is worth a lot of self-pity.'

Robert obeyed, and while he was out in the scullery, Mrs Bostock collected the wrapping paper, and read the note which had given such offense to her troubled son on his fourteenth birthday.

'That money will go towards the camera you want,' she said, when Robert reappeared.

'I'm not so sure about that,' he said mysteriously.

11 ❈ *A Shadow at the Feast* ❈

The entry of the ten piglets into this world must have exhausted them, for the children found them huddled into a heap pressed against the mountainous body of their mother. The whole family were asleep, breathing with great sighs and occasional twitchings, eyes puckered up and tightly closed.

Michael was disappointed. He appealed to the pig-man, who was feeding the mother-to-be in the other sty.

'Which one is going to be mine?'

He was consumed by anxiety.

'You can't tell yet,' said Jennifer. 'Their eyes aren't open. We'll have to wait until the babies are running about.'

Michael leaned over the iron rail and pointed at the panting heap.

'I can see! I can see!' he cried. 'Look! That one with the black spot. That's the one I want. The others are all alike, and I'd never know which is which.'

Mr Bostock, standing behind the children and looking on with amusement at their rapturous excitement, turned to greet his wife and elder son.

'Ah! You've come along, too, Bob! There they are; the ten who have stolen your thunder!'

He put his arm round the boy's shoulder.

'Let them have their hour of glory, son. Look at the pleasure they are bringing with them.'

He indicated the small girl and boy who had not yet noticed the newcomers to the service of adoration.

'They see nothing revolting in it,' whispered Mrs Bostock to him.

'On the contrary, Mary. Just look at the eagerness. They might be watching a miracle.'

'Well, I suppose it *is* a miracle in a way,' she said, but rather dubiously.

'In every way. Don't you agree, Bob?'

But Robert had withdrawn himself from his father's arm. He looked from one to the other of his parents, then at the weltering mass of animal life in the sty.

'I agree with Mother,' he said, and left the party.

He walked down the meadow behind the farm buildings, oblivious of the glory of the April morning, his birthday morning. Primroses and celandine shone in the shadow of the hedgerow, miraculously catching the shafts of sunlight that filtered through the hawthorn and nut bushes. Here and there a blackthorn stood like a little captured cloud, silvery white. Robert was oblivious. He trod down the dandelions in the fresh green grasses. He was lost in his dark mood. Nor did he hear the general hullabaloo of nature, heralding the spring: blackbirds proclaiming their territorial rights; thrushes challenging everything far and wide, three times over; tits, finches, sparrows, robins, chattering and whistling in a general chorus; and, suddenly, hushed and awe-striking through distance—the cuckoo.

Robert heard that last note of derision. He stopped walking and heard it again. His attention was held. He cocked his head to one side, listening more intently. The sound came from somewhere down by the stream where it curved round after leaving the lakes to run through the farm's lower fields, traceable by the oaks, alders, willows and shrubs that lined its banks.

The universal voice of mockery lured him on. He took it as another challenge.

The ground was soft and damp where he approached the stream, and his shoes squelched in mud. He didn't mind that. He was determined to get a sight of that elusive bird. It led him on, ever retreating to another near distance, repeating that double note, hollow and fluty.

Robert's jaw was set as he floundered along beside the stream. The air felt chilly and damp, for the trees were already breaking out of bud and casting a deeper shadow. But Robert's exertion heated him and made him sweat inside his new leather coat. His trousers were muddied as well as his shoes, but he did not care. On he strode, following the lure of that ancient voice. He had no weapon with him, no slingshot, no air gun. He wished he had: but no matter.

He stopped to cut a stick from an ash tree pollarded some seasons ago. The sap was risen in the wood and Robert had only a penknife, none too sharp. The job made him angry with the obstinacy of things, more lasting than the obstinacy of living creatures, but finally he succeeded. By that time, however, the voice had receded into the distance upstream. It fell silent.

But Robert followed on, knowing that the stick was useless, except to make him feel more powerful. He leaped a brook, a tiny tributary between deep banks. Deceived by their slippery sides, quilted under a blanket of golden coltsfoot, he missed his footing and sprawled as he landed. A great smear of clay and pollen disfigured the suede leather of his new coat.

This he *did* notice, and he swore aloud. But he was over the obstacle and trod high through the mass of last year's debris and new vegetation, where the brook met the stream. He was approaching the lower lake now.

Suddenly the cuckoo called again, nearer, louder, more derisive. It was somewhere around the upper lake, that sullen quagmire of reeds and matted rubbish, which had frightened Jennifer and Michael when they tested it at toe point.

Robert pushed on, trying to tread without betraying his approach. He was nearer now. Surely he would see the little brute? He peered as he moved, step by step, one muddy leg after the other. Even the clean-cut ashplant in his hand was mud stained. He looked with dismay at his jacket. The damp stain was growing darker. He blamed the cuckoo. He would make it pay for that.

Suddenly a cloud covered the sun. The April sky tossed and tumbled overhead, and the woods shrank into themselves, veiled and obscure. The air about Robert's heated body grew cold. He shivered and stopped.

So did the cuckoo. It had led him on. Now it was gone and he had not seen it. He saw only the mist lingering over the dead reeds, whiter and whiter as the clouds thickened in the sky.

It was an eerie moment. Robert realized that he had stopped by the treacherous edge where solid land merged into half bog, and the reeds began. He felt uncomfortable and looked down at his muddied clothes. That was bad enough, but there was something more. It was not the mist, now writhing as the wind below the clouds seized it. It was not the sudden coldness. It must be something within himself; a touch of fear, perhaps? He did not wait to find out. He retreated after taking a few steps backward, picking his way as though confronted by an adversary. But there was no adversary:

only the first drops of an April shower, the heaviness of the damp margin, the shiver of his skin inside his soiled jacket, the ashplant in his foolish hand.

He had the sensation of being looked at. He raised the ashplant and waved it around his head and body, but he cut nothing except thin air.

'Silly fool!' he muttered to himself, and immediately realized that he had spoken aloud. He had never done that before and it astonished him. It almost frightened him.

He retreated to firmer ground and easier going. Even so, he felt tired and his legs were heavy as lead.

The sun reappeared. The shower must have fallen farther along the Weald, under the Downs which were still frowning.

Robert looked angrily at the wet stains on his coat, but was sensible enough not to rub them. As he walked, the warm sunlight began to dry them. As soon as one little patch appeared to be dry, he scratched at it with a finger nail. The mud dusted away, leaving only a faint stain. He tried that with his handkerchief and it also disappeared.

Life looked good again; warm and full of birdsong after the lull. The cuckoo began, but miles away now, no longer mocking Robert. Nor was it a solitary voice. Another one, so distant as to be hardly more than a faint echo, answering from another world.

The stains on the suede coat were drying quickly now. Robert scratched some more away. He had a dim feeling of gratitude to his mother and rather reluctantly picked a large bunch of primroses and dog violets to take home to her.

He found her alone in the kitchen, and gave the bouquet to her. She hid her surprise.

'You dear boy,' she said, 'I'll put them on the

middle of the table to mark your birthday luncheon. It's your favorite: steak and kidney pudding. Oh, this wonderful kitchen, with room enough to turn round. It's a joy to work in it!'

She seized Robert and hugged him.

'Fancy! Fourteen today!' she said. Those primroses must have affected her sense of smell. She had buried her nose in them after accepting them from Robert, and her eyes were streaming.

'Ridiculous!' she cried, releasing her son. 'Why, what's happened to the new coat?'

'I slipped down by the brook,' said Robert. He said nothing about his foolish pursuit of the cuckoo, and the uncanny experience by the upper lake.

Mrs Bostock took the coat, and told Robert meanwhile to finish setting the table in the dining room. The primroses spread loosely in a deep dish made a wide moon of color on the table. The violets amongst them added to the lunar effect, as of faintly seen volcanoes.

'Lovely, Bob,' said Mrs Bostock again, as she brushed at the stains on the suede leather with a little rubber brush.

'There, look! Not a mark left!'

This happy *tête-à-tête*, a rare occurrence, was broken by the return of the rest of the family, ravenous with hunger. Jennifer ran to Mrs Bostock with her offering. She, too, had picked a small posy of primroses.

'You too, Jenny?' said her mother. 'I'll have them in front of me on the table. You see, Robert has brought that great mass for the middle.'

'I don't believe it!' said Mr Bostock jokingly.

But Robert took that unkindly. He snatched up the coat from the back of the chair where his mother had hung it after brushing the stains away. He did it so roughly that one of the pound notes fell out of the pocket. Michael pounced on it and handed it to him.

'Huh! Money! Aren't you rich! What are you going to buy with it?'

Robert ignored that. He frowned at his father. 'Thanks for that,' he muttered. His father studied him before replying.

'Splendid, my boy! You'll need a good dictionary now you're fourteen. Time to become articulate. But I'll give you that as well. Spend the money as you wish.'

12 ❖ The Knife ❖

The Sunday passed; the birthday passed. Robert went to bed that night feeling empty, except for a sense of foreboding of something unpleasant likely to happen: a universal experience perhaps, known to everybody: school tomorrow, the office or workshop tomorrow, the same old round, the monotony, the treadmill. Monday morning!

And April blew back to winter, as it does so often for a day or two. The younger children didn't mind the cold rain, for their mother took them to school by car. But Robert had to head against it on his bicycle, struggling to hold down a mackintosh cape against the icy gusts. He reached the Grammar School sweaty and disgusted.

Nothing untoward happened until the session in the gymnasium, before the lunch break. After gym was over and the master departed, a few senior boys carried on, some over the vaulting horse, another little group with the boxing gloves.

Robert was about to leave when one of the second group stopped him.

'Hi, Bossy!' That had become his nickname for obvious reasons. 'We've never seen you with the gloves on. Why is that? Don't you fancy yourself that way?'

The others took it up. 'Come along, Bossy.' 'Let's see how you shape.'

An older prefect joined in. 'Get it out of your system, Bostock. Knock some of these yokels into shape.'

Saying this, he closed the door and stood in front of it. Robert was cornered. He was still the new boy. Since that incident of the bicycle, the practical joke which he had taken badly, suspicion of him had been mounting. Monday morning is a time when such attitudes can take a nasty turn.

Robert found himself being hustled into the center of the group. Gloves were thrust at him.

'I want to go into the town,' he snarled.

'Just a round or two first, Bossy,' said a voice.

'I'll take you on, Bossy,' breathed another in his ear.

Two other boys stripped off his coat, the drab brown tweed uniform that he hated as much as he hated the school; the coat that made him one of the crowd.

There was no way out. He had to show his mettle.

'Don't look too solemn,' said the prefect. 'It's not a duel to the death.'

'Pistols for two, coffee for one,' cried the boy who was putting on the gloves. He gave a dancing step or two in front of Robert, who stood firm, ignoring the fun as he, too, put on the gloves.

'Now then!' said the prefect. 'Clear the ring.'

All the other boys in the gymnasium gathered round. They sensed something unusual.

Robert's opponent was smaller than he: younger perhaps but keen and swift. He was in and out with the attack of a terrier, or an angry wasp.

To begin with, Robert was dazed. He'd done no boxing and his defense was instinctive, at first too low, and he caught several light taps on his face and head.

The round was playful; his opponent's features bright with laughter.

But the mood changed when Robert, dodging another head blow by sidestepping, landed one on the boy's ribs. It made the boy gasp. The laughter was replaced by a look of surprise.

The attack became serious and skillful. Here was an opponent who knew the craft. Nobody had told Robert that he was facing one of the most promising pair of fists in the school team, the pride of the sergeant instructor. This formidable character, formerly of the Buffs, who had boxed for the army, had just reentered the gymnasium, wondering why the boys had not dispersed as usual at lunch hour. He stood watching, behind the ring.

'Keep your gloves up, son,' he said to Robert.

But Robert was not sure what he meant. Another round began and he found himself being attacked seriously. A right and a left got through, and with some power behind them. He was shaken but, at the next attack, repeated the sidestep which he had found useful before. As the glove flashed past, just touching his shoulder, he saw a smear of blood on it. It must be his own blood! He realized that his nose was bleeding: a mere trickle, but it enraged him.

The miss had momentarily thrown his opponent off guard, and Robert saw the small lithe figure about to withdraw, but with a second's hesitation. With all his passionate temper behind the blows, Robert landed a right and left. The one caught the boy in the small of the back; the other in the groin, below the belt. The boy was on the floor, doubled up.

There was a cry of dismay from the ringside. Somebody hissed. The sergeant pushed his way through and seized Robert by the collar.

'Take those gloves off!' he commanded. 'That was not sport. That was a cad's trick! Where d'you come from, some London gutter?'

He turned to the other boy, his young hopeful, and picked him up.

'You never know with beginners,' he said. 'Who is this fellow? I've not seen him here before.'

'Nor will you see me again,' said Robert savagely. 'I didn't start this. These people forced me into it.'

The sergeant studied him for a moment.

'I fancy we *shall* see you again,' he said slowly. 'If we can civilize you, there is the making of a good fighter in you.'

Robert's face ached. His nose must be swollen, for his left eye could see the flesh, though the bleeding had stopped. He stared coldly at the sergeant, then turned and walked out, without a word. The crowd parted to let him through, as it had done after that incident over the bicycle. Silent condemnation is deadly.

Robert walked along the corridor to the washroom and bathed his face in cold water. He saw in the mirror that the damage was hardly apparent. Nor was the damage to his self-esteem; but after the meal, at which again he was left to himself, he walked up into the High Street to the hardware store.

Every town has one such, where the stock sets one longing to spend money. These provincial stores have to cater for farmers, horsy folk, sportsmen, craftsmen, and households. They carry everything from a screw to a motor cultivator; every kind of tool, fitment, replacement; brooms and pans, stoves and electric fittings and light bulbs.

'I want a sheath knife,' said Robert.

'You mean a boy scout's knife and belt?' said the assistant.

'A sheath knife,' repeated Robert, with emphasis.

'Oh, I see; and a stronger belt to go with it?'

Robert nodded. He was led to the back of the shop where the assistant opened the glass-fronted door of a cupboard and invited Robert to explore. Before him lay a variety of knives, from tiny pearl-handled penknives, to massive multiple-bladed instruments, with tiny saws, screwdrivers, several sizes of blade, all folding away into staghorn handles. There were domestic knives, butchers' knives, flick knives and, among them, just the article that Robert had in mind.

It was not too large, but it was a murderous weapon. He drew it from its leather sheath and looked at it, fascinated. He touched the point with the tip of his thumb and it clung to his skin so that he withdrew the touch quickly. He felt the edge. It was hollow-ground, the steel curving down to that edge almost with the illusion of a caress, or a tiny wavelet lapping on the shore with the pressure of the ocean invisible behind it. Robert shuddered; half with joy, half with fear.

'I'll have this one,' he said to the assistant, an elderly man who was studying him with curiosity.

'It's really a huntsman's knife,' he said. 'You need to be careful. Are you sure you—?'

'Thank you,' said Robert coldly.

The assistant said no more and drew several leather belts from the showcase under the counter. Robert liked a broad one, studded with little brass pyramids. That was real armor! But he had spent most of his father's gift on the knife, and he had to be content with a narrow, plain leather belt. But it was practical enough. It could be worn, unseen, beneath his pullover with the sheath knife safely concealed inside the top of his trousers.

He walked back to school for the afternoon session, with confidence renewed. Before going into class, he slunk into a clump of trees behind the cricket pavilion. Nobody was around that shady spot, but he could hear the shouts and cries of people at the nets. Quickly he untied the parcel and put the belt round his waist. Then he attached the knife to it and drew his pullover down. Everything was satisfactory. But before emerging from this secret spot, he had to have another look at his treasure. Peering round the corner of the pavilion, he retreated again into the shadows under the trees, and drew the knife from its sheath.

Its bareness startled him. It looked more dangerous now that he possessed it. He prodded the trunk of a horse-chestnut tree. The blade went in far enough to release a little sap, just a few drops on the naked steel.

Robert wiped its blade with his handkerchief, returned it to the sheath, tugged down the concealing pullover, and joined the boys who were strolling toward the schoolhouses. Nobody spoke to him.

13 ✤ *A Distant Warning* ✤

All through the afternoon session Robert had a feeling of confidence, though aware of being cold-shouldered. He knew what he knew, and spoke up during the usual give and take between boys and masters. One or two of the latter noticed this with surprise. They were accustomed, in their contact with young Bostock, to a reticent character, inclined to be sullen. They were the more surprised because the school grapevine had broadcast the story of Robert's dreadful mistake, through sheer ignorance perhaps, which ended his first, and reluctant, bout in the boxing ring. Words such as 'dirty' and 'cad' had been bandied about, for criticism grows with rumor.

The masters had discussed the incident during their after-lunch chat in the common room, and had agreed that the boy's odd-man-out character, more obvious than first-term awkwardness, was likely to be even more apparent after such an unfortunate show. One or two were sympathetic, and agreed with the physical-training master, the awesome ex-sergeant, that Robert was a dark horse capable of something out of the ordinary. His form master added that it might make him end up in jail.

This conflict of academic opinion was increased by Bostock's assured responses during the afternoon.

He cycled home, buoyed up by that mood. The

April afternoon was warm, and he sweated as he pedaled along the main road and turned into the lane to the castle. Leaning over the handlebars to push up the rise that kept the roar of the twentieth century from that little community of castle, farm, and their cottages, Robert felt the unaccustomed touch of the belt and the knife.

After passing the castle, he found the pressure round his waist beginning to be unbearable. Also the sheath end prodded into his thigh every time his left leg rose. But he was so proud of his secret weapon that he pedaled on, almost enjoying the discomfort.

When he reached the second rise, however, he decided to ease the pressure of the belt, and to move the knife farther round toward his hip, away from the thigh. He dismounted at the bend in the lane, where the land sloped down to the lakes. The freakishly hot air was cooler, coming up from the water and the swamp.

Robert lifted his pullover under his jacket, loosened the belt one notch, and moved the knife three inches along, toward his hip.

'Ah! That's better!' he said aloud, half amused to realize again that he was talking to himself.

But the amusement did not last. Suddenly, he began to shiver. He looked up at the sky. But no, it was warm, blue, ablaze with light. The landscape was filling out visibly. He could have sworn that the green had increased since he rode to school after breakfast. Some hawthorn blossom in the hedges had certainly not been out then. Now it was to be seen, like clots of cream that smelled of almond paste.

But he shivered again, hastily adjusted his pullover and buttoned his coat. Yet still he felt the chill over his skin. It went deeper. It was in his blood and groped at his mind.

He looked down the slope, and saw not so much a mist, as a grayness over the upper lake, forming almost a shape above the masses of withered rushes there. But he was near enough to see that they were less withered. Fingers of green showed through. Somewhere beyond that treacherous life-in-death, the cuckoo was calling again, indolent as a vanishing memory.

A trick of sunlight touched the center of that grayness; drew it together, gave it a shape. Robert saw it. He looked away but looked again, compelled against his will. But the shape was thinning out, nothingness melting into nothingness.

He was still cold, however: an absurd sensation on a warm April afternoon, after hours of sunshine which had drawn life upward from the fields and woods; leaves and flowerets visibly opening, joyous and fragrant.

He put his hand to his mouth. His lips were cold. They were dead, for he could not feel the touch of his fingers on them!

He walked on, pushing his bicycle, too bewildered to mount it. Where the lane curved to the left, to face the forecourt of the castle, he stopped and turned to look back, down the park, to the lakes. He saw nothing unusual. The sunlight glittered on the clear water of the lower lake. It changed the widespread mat of last year's rushes on the upper lake to a glory of gold, arrowed with green from the new shoots. He heard some waterfowl clucking. And the cuckoo was still calling, somewhere in the oak trees beyond the farther bank.

Robert remounted. All was well. The belt no longer constricted him, and the knife lay comfortably close to his hip.

He put his bicycle under cover and was about to go indoors, when he heard his father's voice from the other side of the partition which divided the old stable into two.

'Is that you, Bob? Come and give me your advice!'

Robert went out and leaned over the other stable door. Mr Bostock came forward, blinking at the bright light.

'Ah, son. You're rather late? I'm planning to make myself a workroom of this half, if I throw in that lean-to beyond, and put in a big skylight with a window at the farther end. It's just a bit of a playroom, you know; a relief from modern engineering: back to the village blacksmith and all that. I'll have a furnace and a lathe; of course an anvil. I want to get it all going, for I've a secret plan for Mother's birthday. I intend to make her a pair of firedogs and an iron basket for that naked open hearth in the big room. It's unsafe and wasteful. We shall find, too, that in winter it'll be inclined to smoke. An underdraft will cure that, and—are you listening? Why, anything wrong? You look as though you've seen a ghost!' He laughed. 'Of course, *the* ghost!'

But the laugh died away, and he put his hand on Robert's shoulder and spun him round to the light.

'You're looking odd, my boy. Feeling off color? Why, your face is swollen. Nothing happened at school?'

Robert was annoyed.

'Stop it, Father! Of course not. Gym was a bit strenuous this morning. Some of these country types are pretty rough, too. But I can hold my own. Yes, I can look after myself!'

His father studied him for some moments before replying.

'I see. It's like that, is it? Well, in the long run you've got to stand on your own feet. With that advice,

94

I'll now ask for yours. Come in and help me decide where to place all these fitments. You know how I must have everything shipshape; every tool cleaned and oiled, in its place ready to hand.'

This appeal to his capability pleased Robert. His heart warmed toward his father, and he followed willingly into the dark stable, and had some useful suggestions to offer during the consultation, which Mr Bostock accepted gratefully.

Robert was grateful also, for his father had not pressed the question as to what had happened during the day. Robert appreciated that. It gave him a family feeling; rather a novelty. Even so, during the walk together up to the house, he passed his hand down his hip and felt the reassuring shape of the knife in its sheath.

He went upstairs to his room and changed the detested uniform tweed jacket for the new suede leather coat, his mother's birthday present. He was struggling into it when Michael rushed into the room and seized him round the legs, almost knocking him over. But in his present amiable mood, Robert accepted this as another sign of family affection.

'What's the excitement?' he said. 'Is something on fire?'

'Their eyes are open!' cried the Tyke, thumping into Robert's body. 'Their eyes are open and they are moving about! I'll soon be able to take mine out!'

'What on earth are you talking about?'

But Michael's attention had veered to another matter, just as a butterfly changes its course from one flower to another. He patted Robert's leg.

'What's that?' he said. 'What's that hard lump?'

Robert's kindness vanished. He pushed his young brother away.

'Just you dry up,' he said. 'It's none of your business. You wouldn't understand.'

'But what is it?' Michael persisted. 'Is it secret?'

'Oh, well, I suppose you'll have to know,' said Robert; but he was uneasy.

He put his hand under his pullover and drew the knife from its sheath. This was the first time he had practiced that feat. It was simple and instant. The action pleased him. It was so practical.

'You see that?' he boasted. 'It's a hunting knife. Yes, it is a secret! If you tell, I'll have your head off with it! D'you understand? You're not to say a word!'

He was not sure that Michael understood. The child stood in front of him, staring at the naked blade, hypnotized by the movement as Robert returned it to its sheath.

'But that's deadly,' he whispered, his small face puckered up in bewilderment.

'Of course it is, you ass. That's why you're not to say a word: not a word to anybody, d'you hear?'

Michael nodded gravely.

'Not even Jenny?' he breathed.

Robert had a sensation of trying to cage the west wind. He said no more, and drove the intruder out of his room. Then he settled down to his homework, which was to study *Hamlet*, on which later an essay had to be written. An opening speech caught his attention.

> *Horatio says 'tis but our fantasy,*
> *And will not let belief take hold of him*
> *Touching this dreaded sight twice seen of us—*

He frowned over the words, paused, and read the lines again. They seemed to be familiar; to refer to something that he had experienced. But that was absurd. He did not believe in that sort of rubbish.

96

He was still pondering over it, however, when his mother called up the stairs, summoning her family to the early evening meal.

Parents and children were gathered round the table again, Mr Bostock appreciating his wife's excellent cooking, and the children taking it for granted, as one of the laws of nature. The give and take of conversation persisted over the clatter of plates and cutlery, and the temporary deafness caused by the act of eating.

Robert was anxious. He tried to command Michael's attention by frowning at him from time to time. The device worked, until Jennifer shot one of her seemingly innocent remarks across the table, like a bright silver arrow.

'What are you going to buy with your birthday money, Bob?'

'You shouldn't ask, Jenny,' said her mother, frightened by the silence that followed.

Michael could contain his secret no longer.

'I know!' he cried, his voice shrill with excitement. 'I know! And he's bought it, haven't you, Bob?'

Robert felt four pairs of eyes boring into him. He gulped, fidgeted, glared at Michael, and decided to take a strong stand.

'Oh, well, you might as well know. I've bought *this!*'

He turned up his pullover and awkwardly drew up the knife, careful to keep it in the sheath, to soften the shock.

He heard his mother's exclamation of dismay and was aware of his father's fixed and disapproving stare. But he could not see them. His vision was confused by anger with Michael, and embarrassment because he could not think up a justification which he was willing to reveal.

'Oh, isn't it mighty?' cried Michael. 'Take it out, Bob. Show us the blade.'

His innocence saved the situation. Mr Bostock did not care to criticize Bob in front of the child, and the delay gave him second thoughts: why should he criticize at all?

'Well, you know what you want, Bob. But I can't think why you chose that lethal weapon. We're living in Kent, not the Wild West.'

Bob was emboldened by this tolerance.

'You're living in the past, Dad. Nowhere is safe today.'

His mother was shocked by that.

'Bob, how can you say such things. Where do you get such ideas? Not from home, I'm sure.'

'Except that I shall not feel safe now,' said Jennifer, still in that bland, silvery tone of voice.

'You're a humbug,' retorted Robert, but he was not fierce. He had got over the difficulty of confessing his purchase of the knife more smoothly than he had expected. He looked at his sister almost kindly. All was well. The family dropped the subject, and the dinner-time conversation drifted into more casual matters. Self-confidence returned, and put him off his guard.

14 ❖ The Innocent Eye ❖

Springtime passed into early summer, and during that long school term, the Bostock children, at least Jennifer and Michael, settled into their new way of life contentedly. Indeed, they were more than contented, for everything around them was rich and exciting. Things that country-born children take for granted were miracles for Jennifer and Michael.

The birth of the piglets, for instance: who would imagine that such a natural event held Michael spellbound? He had instantly picked the one from the litter of ten which he claimed as his own. As soon as the hungry little creatures began to run with their dam over the small pasture surrounding the farm buildings, the boy, who was ingenious with his hands, made a tiny harness from a pair of reins, which the piglet accepted with only mild protest. It also accepted the devotion of its self-appointed master and lover.

'And everywhere that Michael went, the pig was sure to go.' It had no alternative, and wore its harness with philosophic grunts, when Michael seized it and led it away from the rest of the litter, and the source of supply. Michael learned quickly not to try its patience for too long at a time. When it grew restive, and inclined to slip out of the harness, he returned it to its mother, but with some reluctance.

No pedigree dog was ever more worshiped than that little runt, with the black spot on its back. When a child of eight concentrates on something with particular enthusiasm, the passion is a consuming fire. Michael ignored the amusement of his parents, the barbed but friendly remarks from Jennifer, and contempt from Robert.

For Robert was not so easily attuned to life at Deepdene Farm and its connections, the castle and the Grammar School. He distrusted this paradise. He wore that belt round his waist, with the handy hunting knife, at home, at school, and wherever he roamed around the farm or farther afield.

He was a lone wolf. His excursions were usually in solitude. He escaped from the family as much as was possible without upsetting the harmony of the household.

Even so, his mother was puzzled.

'John,' she said one night to her husband, after Robert had been out until long after dark, to return with a wary gleam in his eyes, secretive and cautious, 'the boy is still carrying that knife concealed round his waist. What's the object of it? I don't like it.'

'You can't account for the oddities of human nature, Mary. Live and let live is the only way to handle people.'

Mrs Bostock was not comforted.

'Live and let live is all very well, but you don't do it with a murderous knife hidden about your person.'

'Look, Mary. I'm the one who usually criticizes him. I realize it was becoming a bad habit, though he asks for it. He's of an age when we must leave him alone, to spread his wings.'

They said no more, except that they were thankful the two younger children were still of an age when all the world was wonderful, no matter how they pulled it about, and messed it up with their clumsy eagerness.

Mrs Bostock took a parting shot, before turning out her bedside lamp.

'If only he would believe in something; show some interest!'

'Wait, my dear, wait,' said her husband drowsily.

Robert appeared to be waiting, too, though the lack of interest was hardly a fair accusation. He was interested enough in the castle library, of which Mr Culverton had given him the freedom. Many of Robert's absences from home were due to that attraction on summer evenings and at weekends.

That formidable person evidently liked the boy, and offered no objection when Robert asked if he might sometimes bring his homework and do it there. Sometimes became often. The books in the library attracted him, too. He found a lot of strange stuff. One of the founders of the library must have had an interest in the darker side of knowledge: necromancy, black magic, medieval superstitions. Robert caught on to that sort of thing with avidity. It drew him as a magnet draws iron.

He found the little book again; the book written and printed locally, in Cranehurst, in execrable print on rough paper. Its binding looked as though it did not belong to it. A tiny bead of dried glue came away when Robert opened it. Probably it had been loosened weeks ago, when Mr Culverton took the book from the shelves to read to Robert about the ghost of Deephurst Castle, but told more of the story than he read from the book.

The little bead of glue startled Robert. He picked it up from the carpet, and studied it guiltily, as though he might have been trying to steal something, or had broken a precious object. It was hard as a crystal. It was neither brown nor red. It could have dropped from another world; so Robert imagined. His mind had grown wings since he had been introduced to the library at Deephurst Castle and the powerful personality of Mr Culverton, the bachelor hermit living alone there.

Robert no longer dismissed ideas that he did not understand. He read the story of the French lieutenant again. It was clumsily told, by somebody not accustomed to writing books. The author was probably a person in the village, hoping to sell the pamphlet to visitors to Cranehurst Church and what were then the castle ruins; maybe a hundred years ago. But because it was so crudely written, and equally crudely printed and bound, the effect was all the more compelling. It made the story so original, so firsthand, like a bit of papyrus unearthed by an archaeologist from an ancient tomb.

Robert read it again, then furtively put the book back in its place. He read no more that evening, but sat for half an hour at his homework. He made little head-way there either. Finally, he gave up and cycled home to dinner. He knew that he would be late, and that some caustic remark would register the fact. But he could not hurry. He was oddly tired. School had not been too good during the day. He still had no friends there. The sum-mer term was drawing toward the long holidays, with Sports Day, and tea for parents on the lawn of the School House, where the headmaster lived. Robert had met that august figure only once, when joining the school. The headmaster was old, and evidently had no curiosity left toward the present-day pupils. Generation after generation had passed through his hands, and he had had enough; especially if a new boy appeared sulky and hostile, with no marked ability.

That might have been another reason why young Bostock was left alone. Masters and boys did not exactly send him to Coventry, but they walked round him.

He was thinking about this as he pedaled home-ward. The summer evening was damp, but warm. All manner of rich smells floated in the air: honeysuckle, the whiff of cut hay still in bales ungathered from one huge field, a sweetness of cows in a meadow nearer home, the roses in the garden and up the walls of the farmhouse.

As he rode round to the stables, he looked up at the attic, with the little dormer windows. Even from ground level he could see, faintly, the gray markings on that diamond pane, like a blind eye. It gave him the sensation of being reminded of something; of being followed.

He was not late for the meal, after all. Mr Bostock had been up to London, and was only just returned. So the parents and Robert sat down together. Jennifer and Michael had been fed earlier, and were out of doors for a while before their bedtime.

'Father, Mr Culverton said he wanted to see that signature on the window in the attic,' said Robert.

'When was this, son?'

'Oh, weeks ago: when we first came here.'

'Why on earth didn't you tell us before?'

'I forgot. It's awful rot really. But he did say he thought it was important.' Then Robert added, but not sincerely, 'I can't think why.'

He knew that this was not true. He knew that, inside himself, something was changing since he had come to live at the farmhouse. He frowned and added angrily, 'You see, I don't believe in all that nonsense!'

His father looked at him in surprise.

'You need not be so emphatic, Bob. Nobody's driving you to it.'

'Oh, aren't they?' exclaimed Robert.

Before the startled parents could respond, their attention was diverted by the return of Jennifer.

'He's got the baby pig with him! I said he ought to take it back to the rest, but he's bringing it into the house!'

'Oh, my dear,' cried Mrs Bostock. 'The child is possessed! I must go. He'll need persuading. They get all this obstinacy from you, John. I'm sure I'm not made that way.'

She retreated to the kitchen, where she found Michael kneeling over his pet, for whom he had poured out at least a pint of milk into a bowl. He was reverently counting every snort, every guzzle, as the milk disappeared.

'Oh, Michael, *must* you?' cried his mother.

He did not hear. His attention was wholly given to the little flesh-pink body with the black spot. When the milk at last disappeared, he sighed with relief, and looked up at his mother.

'He loves that,' said Michael. 'He doesn't get enough with all those others to push him away.'

Mrs Bostock blushed. She was not sure that she liked the small boy's concentration on such maternal matters.

'Well, dear, you must take him back to the sty now. Bedtime for both of you!'

'Yes, I suppose so,' he replied rather sadly. He was thoughtful.

'He *could* sleep in a basket in our room, you know.'

'Good heavens! What would Robert say?'

'Well, can't you give Bob another room? There are plenty in this house.'

'But what about you sleeping alone?'

'I shouldn't be alone. I should have Herbert with me.'

104

'Herbert? Whoever is Herbert?'

She thought the child must be referring to an imaginary companion.

'That's his name,' Michael drew the piglet to him. The creature, stupefied with so much food, made no objection. It merely staggered a little under the passionate embrace.

'I christened him Herbert.'

'Wherever did you get that name? There are no Herberts in the family.'

'That's why: because he's not like anyone else.'

Mrs Bostock succeeded in not laughing. She ruffled the small boy's hair.

'Come along, then. I'll walk with you up to the sties. But why did you have to pick this one out especially? There are nine others, and seven with the other sow.'

Michael glanced at her scornfully and did not deign to reply. He marched solemnly, with Herbert in the lead and on the lead, to the back door, the piglet apparently recovered from its coma and eager for another and more natural meal.

Daylight outlined the matter-of-fact procession: Herbert, Michael, followed by Mrs Bostock. The sun burned low in the north-west and Mrs Bostock shielded her eyes with her hand. The white hoods of the hop kilns shone, clean-cut against the sky.

'Oh, what a night!' she said. 'Heaven on earth.'

'It's not night. The sun's still shining,' said Michael without looking back at her. He was too preoccupied with his pet.

'Well, it's bedtime, anyway. So hurry up now. That's right, put him in quickly and shut the hatch before some of the others rush it and escape. And you shall have a room of your own.'

But mother pig and the nine were inside the sty, one large coagulation of slumber.

Michael slipped the harness off Herbert's plump body and pushed him through the hatch. With a squeal of satisfaction, the favored one rushed under cover to rejoin his family. The disturbance roused the others, squeals and grunts rose, the mother snorted and rolled over, scattering progeny round the open pen. They ran about protesting, then reassembled to cluster at the welcoming dugs, Herbert foremost.

Michael, now reassured, took his mother's hand, content to return to the house and his own bed. But first Mrs Bostock gave him a bath, for he smelled rather strong. When she had tucked him up for the night, she leaned over the sleepy figure, now dim in the gathering twilight. He put his hand up to touch her face.

'Herbert *is* mine, isn't he?'

'We all belong to each other, Mike. That's how it is. So now go to sleep.'

She left him and went to her own bedroom, surprised by a spasm of fear. She lingered until it had passed, and she could rejoin the rest of the family downstairs.

15 ❖ *The Signature Again* ❖

Mr Culverton was invited to dinner a few days later. Now that royalties from the patent were rolling in, Mrs Bostock was able to show her qualities as a cook. Mrs Green was in attendance, voluble and willing. Delicious smells floated around the kitchen, slightly salty, with a suspicion of garlic, damp salads, the nutty bouquet of Marsala wine, the savor of homemade *pâté*.

Mrs Green set the table. She had not forgotten her training as a parlor maid up at the castle, in the days before the war, when parlor maids were not yet extinct. She polished up the antique silver and the Waterford wine glasses which Mrs Bostock had brought to the marriage contract. The table gleamed in depth. It suggested ancestors. Nobody would have believed that only a few months ago the Bostock family was huddled anxiously in a suburban London villa, with the wolf of uncertainty at the door.

On the day of the dinner party, Mr Bostock went with Mr Culverton to the London office of the great firm. They traveled back together, and Mr Culverton stopped off at the castle, while his host for that evening drove on to the farmhouse, with a great sheaf of rose-buds, glorious, deep-glowing Ena Harkness buds, to surprise his wife with this sign of good fortune and the importance of the occasion.

She did not fail to appreciate the gesture and Mr Bostock was duly rewarded, as attentive husbands can be rewarded. The flowers, brought from London to the country, looked all the more rare and sophisticated, but they lacked the lavish perfume of the bowlful from the garden, which was now displaced from the center of the table and relegated to the side dresser, where the two decanters of Bordeaux wine smoldered and flared, as people passed to and fro in front of them.

Mr Culverton arrived at the farmhouse with Robert whom he had found in the library at the castle. They cycled down together, talking as they pedaled.

'You know your father has invented one of those simple things which ought to have been discovered by the ancient Egyptians?' said Mr Culverton. 'We saw some figures at a board meeting today. They showed how his little device can save any power plant about twenty-five percent of its fuel costs. It's a stroke of genius, you know! I hope you appreciate your father, Robert?'

'Why not?' said Robert dryly.

'Well, prophets in their own country!'

They pushed on for half a mile, over the second hillock in silence. Then Mr Culverton attacked again.

'It took me a long time to realize what my own father had done to build up the vast concern which I now have to direct.'

Robert did not reply. He had the suspicion that he was being criticized, and what with life at Cranehurst School and his father's frequent jibes, he felt he had enough to put up with. Moreover, he had believed that Mr Culverton was a friend who understood him.

'What have I done?' he blurted out at last, and aggressively.

'I wouldn't know,' replied Mr Culverton. 'You're

108

not a very communicative fellow, are you, Robert? If I were asked to give you a reference for the job of Prime Minister, I should be inclined to say that you carry a chip on your shoulder. The weight of that prevents you from noticing what other people have to lump around.'

He left Robert to consider this for a while, as the hedgerows flowed past them, and the farmhouse hove in sight, behind a whole city of blue spires—delphiniums and belated lupins. Then he added, 'My word! Your garden is a lovely sight! That's your mother's work, I suppose?'

Still Robert was silent. When they dismounted, however, he took Mr Culverton's bicycle, a battered old object, and wheeled it with his own round to the barn, while his parents came out to greet the guest.

'You've worked a miracle here, Mrs Bostock,' said the formidable figure who walked between man and wife into the house.

'Oh, I love it all,' was her reply. 'I can't begin to tell you—'

He looked at her seriously, and spoke with slow deliberation.

'That son of yours will do you great credit one of these days, Mrs Bostock. You may be anxious about him but these awkward colts often become good runners.'

Mrs Bostock was startled. She hardly knew Mr Culverton and was not prepared for his sudden plunge into personal intimacies, even though they implied praise.

'Are we anxious about him, John?' she said, appealing to her husband. But he dodged that, and handed glasses of sherry to her and Mr Culverton, the latter still pondering on something he wanted to say. It was also to the point.

'Of course you're anxious. So should I be if I were

a parent and had a cub as antisocial as that lad of yours. But never fear. Mark my words! He has a future, or I'm no judge of character.'

'What makes you think that?' said Mr Bostock rather sharply.

But Robert appeared from the back of the house, and the conversation became general.

The dinner was a great success. Mr Culverton appreciated the good claret and said so. He was a forthright person, who spoke with authority and ignored conventional small talk.

'Well, I came not only to enjoy your hospitality, my dear Bostocks. I'm really intrigued by Robert's discovery of that bit of historical evidence on the window pane in the attic here. May we go and inspect?'

'Yes, there's still daylight enough,' said Mr Bostock. 'But what does it signify?'

Only the two men and the boy went up. None of them noticed the door of Jennifer's room open an inch or two after they had passed, and a shrewd little face peering out.

The dormer faced westward, and the sky beyond it was a glory of color that touched the white scratchings on the pane, making them by contrast spidery and otherworldly. Mr Culverton touched them with his forefinger.

'Yes,' he murmured to himself. 'Yes, that is the man: Raymond de Crétien. Poor devil! He got roughly handled; and only a few months before the whole lot were released and shipped back to France after peace was patched up. D'you know the story, Bostock? Has Robert told you?'

Mr Bostock looked inquiringly at his son, who turned aside in confusion, because he was suddenly reminded of Mr Culverton's words during the ride up from the castle, suggesting that he did not show any interest in his father, or confide in him.

But nothing would induce Robert to talk about ghosts.

'Father's an engineer,' he said. 'He wouldn't be interested in spooks.'

'You warned me yourself, Culverton, before we came to live here.'

Mr Bostock was covering up for Robert. He turned to him now. 'Don't you remember, Bob? When we drove up, on the day we moved, I told the whole family that we were likely to have a regular visitor from time to time.'

'Yes, but you were joking.'

To the surprise of both father and son, Mr Culverton broke in with some irritation.

'Yes, my boy. Your father's an engineer; and I'm a man of business. But let me tell you this. I wish to God this poor fellow's soul could rest in peace!'

He shook his hands nervously in front of his face, and turned away to hide his feelings by staring closely at the elaborate signature scratched two hundred years ago on that little leaded pane of glass.

He recovered instantly and stepped back to rejoin the others, who stood silent and embarrassed. He put a hand on Robert's shoulder and shook him vigorously.

'How old are you, Robert? Thirteen, fourteen? You've a lot to learn before you can begin to doubt.'

He turned to Mr Bostock. 'I'm glad to have seen that. It may explain why the young man broke out for a couple of weeks. Another character who couldn't mix, eh, Bostock? And probably he added to that by getting caught up in an affair with the farmer's daughter who was working up at the castle. That again would have ended in disaster; for the girl at least. There were class differences in those days, as well as national divisions. But let us go down!'

He was the formidable Mr Culverton again, leading the way, followed by his host.

Robert was shaken by the power of this man's character, which had been attacking him, as he believed, all evening from the moment when Mr Culverton found him in the library at the castle and proposed the bike ride together, on to the dinner party at the farmhouse.

Robert stayed behind in the attic, his mind confused. He was resentful, because he had been the object of Mr Culverton's onslaught. He was puzzled, because such an impressive person could take all this nonsense about a ghost so seriously.

The sunset was dying down and the little diamond panes in the attic window grew somber, like stained glass; smoky red, then purple, with the scratched signature of Raymond de Crétien fading into a gray smudge.

Robert watched its near extinction, paler and paler. An after-sunset movement of the air sighed across the world, adding to the sense of loneliness, of departure. It lipped at the loose-fitting leads of the dormer. Robert heard it: a faint moan. He saw its effect on the ground mist across the farm, where the stream flowed. He watched the mist mold itself into a shape, a tall figure, that moved in front of the woods across the stream: a tall figure, thin, and with one arm outstretched, pointing at something, or beckoning.

Robert shuddered. That made him angry with himself, and he left the attic hurriedly.

16 ✤ 'Into a Dark and Lonely Wood' ✤

That colorful sunset foretold good weather, and the following week was a glorious example of what high summer can be. The sun blazed, day after day, and the barley grew almost visibly, lifting the fields and making them seem smaller. The trees thickened, and the woods turned a darker green.

Windows of the farmhouse were open night and day, for the Bostocks, being townfolk, had the illusion that in the country there was no need to lock up at night. This innocent trust in Nature affected Mrs Bostock, Jennifer, and Michael. They might have been living in fairyland, or the Garden of Eden. They clung together, did things together, nearly always out of doors around the farm, or in the woods across the castle park. Michael was reluctant to go too far afield because Herbert, his own and beloved piglet, was a wayward traveler, even in harness, and obstinately refused to venture far from the sty and the unfailing supply of nourishment.

Michael's enthusiasm in this matter, his passionate devotion, amused his mother and even Jennifer. Maternal instinct is infectious, especially when so abundant, as it was during those early weeks in the two sties behind the big barn. Why Michael, a small boy brimful of mischief, should have been captivated is one of life's mysteries impossible to explain.

He became quite pathetic with protective responsibility. Herbert was his sole interest in life.

'That kid is mad,' said Robert. It was an abrupt remark made on the Saturday afternoon after the week of hot days. The family, with the exception of the Tyke, were sitting out under a great cedar tree on the lawn in front of the farmhouse. Mr Bostock was reading a book, with intervals of dozing. Mrs Bostock stitched half-heartedly at garments in need of repair. Jennifer lay on her stomach, doing nothing, her school books scattered around her. She was not even daydreaming, for her brother's interruption of the silent hour instantly prompted her: 'Boys don't go mad at his age. It doesn't happen until they're fourteen.'

Father looked up. Mother looked up, startled.

'What's that?' said Mr Bostock.

'Your brilliant daughter,' said Robert sarcastically.

'Now, Robert,' said his mother, quite unjustly; probably confused by the heat. 'Don't start bickering.'

Robert was so aggrieved by this injustice that he left the peaceful circle and strolled away, out of sight. He was bored. He did not share the contentedness of the family. He found the weekend dull, in spite of the superb weather and the glory of the garden and countryside. He was depressed, too, because the past week at school had been worse than usual: the hot classrooms, the clammy textbooks, the mania for cricket, and the continued, unspoken hostility toward him.

He pondered whether or not he should cycle up to the castle. The library would be cool. He was also half hopeful of meeting Mr Culverton. He did not know why, for an encounter with that formidable person would probably end in his being crushed. Yet even so, Robert had the sensation of being understood by this man, as by nobody else.

Also, he wanted to escape from something. It was absurd but he still believed he was being followed about, no matter where he might be: at school, at home, or roaming in solitude through the woods and meadows.

He was glad he had bought that knife: at least, he told himself that he was glad. He felt it against his hip as he walked up to the barn to fetch his bicycle.

All was quiet around the farm buildings. The cows were out, three fields away, standing or lying down, their coats sleek and silken under the caress of summer. Tails flicked at flies, jaws ruminated. A few starlings fidgeted round the somnolent beasts. But even the birds appeared to feel the heat.

The barn door had been left open, and the sunlight glittered on Robert's bicycle, which leaned against a beam in the full glare. The seat almost seared his backside when he set off down the drive and along the lane. He saw his mother look up from her sewing to wave to him, and Jennifer raised one leg into the air and dropped it again. Mr Bostock made no sign. He was lost in his book.

Robert looked back at the family group, as it grew smaller. Something about his father's indifference angered him; as always. He pedaled on, switching to low gear, to save effort, for he was in no hurry. Time had to be killed, anyway. He was not sure that he wanted to read.

He was so preoccupied, or so languid in the heat, that he almost collided with a tractor coming back to the farm. The young man driving it grinned and shouted.

'Wake up, Bobby! What you dreaming about?'

He wasn't very friendly. Robert found few people friendly. That was why he was out on the heat-shimmering road at this moment, drawing nearer, possibly, to the one person who *was* friendly toward him, but in a scarifying way: Mr Culverton.

Robert rode on, and at the bend, came within sight of the top of the castle tower ahead, and, beyond the hedge to his left, the sloping parkland and the lakes.

It was an empty landscape, except for one small figure, conducting a still smaller one. Michael was tacking across the grass toward the end of the lower lake, where the woods took over. He seemed to be having some difficulty with his navigation; indecisive stops, rushes to right and left, wayward changes of pace.

Robert dismounted at a gate into the field, and watched his young brother. He shouted to him.

'Hi! What on earth are you doing?'

Then he saw that Michael's progress was hindered by tears. Michael was a tough character, not prone to tears though only eight years old. The sight was so unusual that Robert decided to investigate.

He climbed over the gate, and joined the habitually infuriating young brother.

'What's wrong?' he said roughly, but less unkindly than usual.

'It's Herbert,' replied Michael brokenly. 'I want to take him to the woods for his first long run. Pigs like acorns but he won't come.'

'He's telling you, stupid! There are no acorns yet. They don't appear until autumn.'

Before Michael could respond, the unwilling Herbert, with a little squeal of triumph, slipped his harness and was off toward the lake like a miniature rhinoceros.

The chase was on! Michael was handicapped both by his tears and by his surprise. He stood staring, still quivering with sobs, mainly of exhaustion, for he had been struggling with the obstinate animal all the way from the farm, coaxing and tugging. The lost moments put him out of the race, and he willingly left it to Robert, who commanded him to 'Wait there. I'll carry it home.'

Herbert was approaching dangerously near to the lake. Robert, worried by the child's distress, changed his instruction.

'You go back home,' he shouted over his shoulder. 'I'll catch the . . .' But he did not waste more breath, for Michael, tired out and docile, was for once obedient.

'Wheel my bike back,' shouted Robert, during a momentary pause as he saw Herbert hesitate about what direction to take.

It was fun at present. Robert had taken the reins from Michael's hands, and he waved them above his head, like a lasso. This reminder of captivity set Herbert off again and on a different course. He veered to the end of the lake, making for the wood to which he had refused to be taken under his loving master's guidance.

Robert ran toward the wood, to cut him off before he could take cover. The quarry was overtaken just in time and Robert felt a surge of triumph. But it was premature.

Herbert displayed the agility and cunning of a First Division center forward. Just as Robert stooped to snatch him up, he doubled back and dodged, and in a second was again out of reach, still heading for the shelter of the trees. In that close moment, Robert realized how the little beast had grown during the summer. The promise to 'carry it home' was likely to be more than he had bargained for. But of course it was a simple matter.

He became more earnest, more intent. This was other than a bit of fun.

'Blast you!' he muttered.

Then Herbert reached his goal, and was marked only by the waving of undergrowth: bracken, ferns, wild garlic, and other woodland green, which parted and closed again behind the vigorous little body, now invisible beneath it.

Robert entered the half light under the trees, and stood for a few moments while his vision grew accustomed to it, after the glare outside.

Then, some yards farther in, where a beech tree stood with bare soil beneath it, Herbert broke cover and halted. He was interested in the layer of last year's husks, and sampled a mouthful. Robert crept toward him, lifting his legs over the undergrowth and the trailers of bramble. He was wearing sandals and his feet suffered. One hidden bramble shoot almost tripped him, and its spines drew blood from his ankle. It hurt, and he muttered 'Damn,' blaming Herbert.

But he reached his greedy little quarry, who was still engrossed in the discovery of the odd nut. Their age and dryness did not deter him. Robert heard the *munch-munch* of the maturing little jaws at work. He saw the sly glance from those glittering eyes, calculating his approach.

The shrewdness of that glance, half defiant, half derisive, made Robert more aware of his torn skin. It rubbed salt into the wounded ankle. His temper began to rise, but he recognized this weakness and tried to remain calm.

That was a new experience, begun since he had become friendly with Mr Culverton; if it can be said that one could become friendly with that unpredictable person. There was also this other influence: the sensation of being watched, of being followed. Even though Robert told himself that this was absurd, it made him study himself and wonder about these outbursts of rage that made him hate the whole world. So now he held himself back. He kept calm.

Herbert munched on, still studying the situation out of those cunning little eyes.

Then Robert jumped, to throw himself on the little beast and grasp it in his arms.

A loud squeal of protest—and Herbert was gone!

Robert lay sprawled and empty-handed. He felt pain down his thigh, where the knife in its sheath had pressed against his body.

'You little devil!' he said, half laughing, half angry.

He scrambled up, and saw that Herbert had merely removed himself to the other extreme of the beech mast carpet! Such indifference was both challenging and contemptuous.

It was too much for Robert. For a moment he stood rubbing his leg to ease the pain. Instinctively his hand touched the knife handle, and without thought or constraint he drew the blade.

He approached Herbert, step by step. His lips were trembling. So was his hand on the knife.

The piglet, emboldened by success, or intoxicated by the pleasure of his newly-discovered feast, tried a new tactic. He suddenly dashed straight at Robert, to escape between the boy's legs. What happened next was so quick and unpremeditated that Robert himself was unaware of it. It was one of those instantaneous events that can never be made clear as evidence in a court of law.

There lay Herbert, just behind Robert, with the lifeblood gushing out from a long wound behind the neck and along the spine. Had the piglet impaled itself on the knife? Had Robert, overcome by one of his moods of sulky rage, deliberately stabbed the adversary at the moment of bravado?

A dreadful silence followed. It seemed to Robert that the whole universe paused, while he stared at the dying animal, the dead animal.

The knife in his hand appeared to be clean; but his wrist was wrenched and his fingers numb. He stared at the blade, then again from the corpse to the guilty hand, unable to think, unable to comprehend. There *was* blood on the blade.

Then, from somewhere by the lakeside, farther off by the upper lake, a green woodpecker broke into its derisive laughter. It was a fiendish sound, breaking over the silence of the sleepy landscape.

Robert moved away a little, knelt and cleaned his knife, deliberately not looking at it. He plunged it into the soft cushion of beech mast, up and down, up and down several times, and fiercely, to remove possible stains, and also possible blame.

He left the knife upright in the ground, then suddenly he put his hands to his face, and shook with sobs. This reaction lasted for only a few moments. He recovered but only to a sort of numbness of mind, and acted as though in a dream world. He wiped the blade of his knife, examining it closely; not a sign of blood.

He returned it to the sheath as he stood up. The mocking laughter of the woodpecker woke him from this half-dazed state of mind. He looked around. Of course, there had been no witness; no sign of Michael.

But what about Michael? What was he to be told? Robert had no ready answer. He turned to action, by dragging the piglet away from the scene of the murder. He hid it below the undergrowth near the base of an oak tree nearby. He plucked some bracken fronds and added them to the cover.

His mind was still numb. The anger, the rage, had

left it bruised. He found himself wondering why he was marking the spot by bending and breaking a bough of the oak tree, so that the place could easily be found again. Who was to find it? Himself?

He came out of the wood, into the sunlight, and walked slowly across the sward to the gate, where he had left his bicycle. It was still there, though he had told Michael to wheel it home. Robert wondered about that, but again found no answer.

If he rode home, he would find Michael. What then? He stood by the gate, sweating after his exertions, under the heat of the afternoon sunlight, which glared both from the sky and from its reflection in the lower lake and lancelike breaks in the matted rushes of the upper lake.

He found himself walking toward the water. He did not want to go there, but could not resist. His legs were not his own legs. His body was possessed by some willpower other than his own. He had the illusion that he could still hear Michael weeping. Never before had he noticed other people's emotions.

'It was not my fault,' he muttered aloud, and then realized that he was talking to himself. It was becoming a habit.

He went on like a sleepwalker, and reached the clear water of the lower lake. He stopped and stared into the glaring reflection, hurting his eyes. The surface was dappled with circles where fish leaped. He spoke aloud again, his eyes closed against the accusing fire of the sun.

'You can't blame me. I don't know what happened!'

Another voice answered. He was quite sure it was another voice. It came from that dimmed confusion of light, passing through his eyelids and colored by them as by a blood-red curtain. It came from a distance, the upper lake; the desolate stretch dominated by bulrushes, their somber brushes deadly still, like a waiting regiment.

The voice was coldly impersonal, indifferent to Robert's dilemma. But it was urgent and anguished.

'Bury my bones,' it entreated. 'But bury my bones.'

Robert froze. Fear crept over his skin. He opened his eyes and the summer rushed at him again, fierce as a tiger! He was weak against this strength; the strength of the earth, the sun, and something else, something behind what he could see, hear, smell, touch. That something commanded him again. 'Bury my bones.' It repeated the plea, moaning into silence, then rising again, as wind rises and falls round a ruin.

Robert lifted his hands and looked at them, doubting if they were real.

'No!' he whispered. 'No.' His voice was not his own voice. He did not recognize it. Some dreadful change was taking place. He was in another world; a world on fire, but icy cold; a world that was waking him, drawing him on but also destroying him.

He must escape from this ferocity of light beating up from the clear water, or he would be blinded. He stumbled along the edge of the lake, shielding his eyes with his half-closed fingers. Reaching the upper lake, he dared to look openly at the close ranks of the bulrushes.

Then he saw it.

Somewhere, but not anywhere, he saw the shape molded out of nothingness, or perhaps the dampness above the matted clots of growth from vanished years. It was a grayish figure, seemingly wearing a full-length dark blue coat. But all was semitransparent, deceptive. Yet a face was visible; or rather a skull. An arm rose, moved forward, as though to point at Robert. But it fell again, and vanished. The whole experience was less substantial than a rainbow; but it was personal, it directed itself at Robert, demanding something from him, urgently, fiercely, yet with utter despair, utter hopelessness.

Then the apparition was gone. The summer afternoon denied it. Sunshine and the bosomy earth surrounded Robert, where he stood trembling, broken.

Slowly he came back to himself, and in that restoration of his willpower he stepped back a few paces, then found the courage to turn and walk away. The field seemed vast, for his limbs were not yet under control. Nature had been reversed, mocked, denied. Robert was newly returned to his own body, and incredulous of it; incredulous of everything.

He began to disbelieve what he had seen and heard. But there the experience stood in his memory, as solid an event as the death of the piglet, and the grief that was coming to young Michael.

Robert mounted his bicycle and began to ride home. But suddenly he stopped, dismounted, turned back, leaned the machine against the gate, and deliberately retraced his footsteps to the upper lake.

There on the spot where he had stood during the apparition, he unfastened his belt and withdrew it from his waist. The knife in its sheath flapped against his leg. He looked at it for a moment, and saw that the handle still carried a small stain of blood.

But now he was in command of himself. He no longer spoke aloud. He was resolute. Gathering all his strength, he whirled the belt and its weapon round his head three times, and sent it flying.

It soared like a meteor, flashing in the sun, the dagger first, the belt trailing behind. The arc ended in the middle of the lake, where that figure had formed in the semidarkness of the bulrushes. He saw the knife go down through the rushes, through the mat of debris, dragging the belt with it. A stain of black water marked where the intrusion had disappeared. Then the weeds and wreckage closed again, and all was as it had been before.

Robert did not wait. He remounted his bicycle, and rode back to the farmhouse.

17 ❖ 'Too True to Be Good' ❖

Robert saw the family still under the cedar tree on the lawn: but no longer peaceful. All were on the lookout with Michael standing on the small table from which the tea tray had been removed to a chair.

As soon as Robert appeared in sight, Michael shouted, leaped from the table, and came running to the gate. Both parents rose to their feet, and Jennifer scrambled up to follow Michael.

'Where is he? Where is he?' cried Michael.

Robert dared not hesitate. But he could not look at his brother. He addressed himself to Jennifer, challenging her quick wits.

'He's still in the wood!'

It was a simple thing to say. And it was the truth. But there was once an occasion when Pilate the Judge asked 'What is truth?'

Robert's answer had fallen like a stone.

'He's lost?'

The child's question was equally heavy. It was flung back at Robert, and it hurt him.

'He's lost,' he repeated.

This again was truth. But Robert knew that he was playing for time. What had been happening to him down in the woods, and during the confrontation by the lakes, was still happening to him.

The dreadful awakening! He knew that he was something other than his former self; something *more* than that self. He had learned to be afraid. But he must not show it!

He watched Michael crumple. The small figure trembled and gathered into itself. Tears flowed, sobs shook his body. Jennifer gathered him to her, but she looked Robert in the face. Her eyes accused him. He knew what they meant. They meant 'Liar!'

But he braved it out. She of all people must not know what he had done. The tumult and revolution raging within him rendered him defenseless, in a world suddenly enlarged, exploding into realities beyond unreality, voices crying in his brain that he knew nothing, had not even begun to understand what he had believed to know so well, and could command by his pride and the threat of his hunting knife.

The knife was gone. But he still had his pride. That should not be snatched from him. He must guard it!

'Well,' he said, frowning at Jennifer, 'it can't be helped.'

But Mr Bostock, taking Robert's bicycle from him, spoke quietly.

'Take him to Mother, Jenny. You look fagged out with the heat, Robert. Go and have some tea. I'll put your machine away. Later on we'll search the wood.'

The kindness was as cruel as Jennifer's silent accusation.

'It rushed toward the lake,' said Robert. Truth still prevailed, and his father accepted it, interpreting Robert's words as a gentle means of breaking the bad news to Michael.

Michael, however, rebelled against the father's effort to calm things down, and to delay further proceedings while Robert refreshed himself from what remained on the tea tray.

'He'll fall in the lake!' cried Michael, struggling out of his mother's arms, to which Jennifer had passed him.

'We must find him now. A fox will get him. Or he may go out to the road and be run over. Daddy, please!'

He started off, no longer crying, but purposeful. His father and brother had to follow and Jennifer seized Robert's bicycle, overtaking them in the lane, standing on one pedal and treading the ground with her right foot. She was soon away in front, and by the time Mr Bostock and the boys reached the gate into the park, Jennifer was seen across the open greensward, disappearing into the wood.

Robert sweated with anxiety. He led the way farther north, as remote as possible from the tell-tale spot. He shouted to Jennifer, urging her with word and gesture to join them. But she took no notice, and went her own way. He gave up, hoping against hope that she would find nothing.

'He'll bear toward home,' he said. 'That's instinctive!'

The others followed him, and they entered the wood where it spread round, after leaving the lower lake behind the fields lying to the right of the land on its way to the farmhouse.

The heat was still intense, and Robert felt it. So did his father. The air beneath the crowded trees was twilit and fragrant, but it seemed no cooler. Indeed, it was damp and dense, which added heaviness to the heat.

'Bob, I can't rove about like this,' gasped Mr Bostock after being led deliberately astray in the wood for nearly half an hour, with Michael tagging along doggedly behind, making forays to right and left, tiring himself with calling 'Herbert! Herbert!' monotonously, and with no success.

'D'you hear? We're surely near the northern end of the wood. We'll break out and cut across to the farm. You, for one, have done enough for today!'

Robert was too weary to be startled by the double truth of that last remark. But his ruse had worked. His father and Michael were safely conducted away from the spot where Herbert lay, lightly covered with beech mast and a few bits of bracken.

Michael, also, was flagging. His voice no longer piped through the silence of the wood, to be baffled by the trees. Herbert's refusal to hear, or to return to him, began to affect his loyalty. Or it may have been exhaustion that made him lose interest.

'Let's go home,' he said sadly. He shed a few tears again, leaning against his father, who patted him fondly to comfort him.

'Never mind, Mike. If your little friend doesn't turn up, we'll have to find you another one.'

'I don't want another one. I want Herbert!'

The mere suggestion of total loss set him off into a paroxysm of grief, and his father picked him up and carried him out into the open sunlight, away from the ominous, brooding shadows of the woods.

Robert followed. He, too, was gloomy, no longer pleased with his success in putting the others off the scent. And he was puzzled. What puzzled him was that Michael's grief affected him, and upset him. Never before had he been conscious of other people's feelings, except as a threat or a challenge.

'Damn!' he said to himself. He was angry about that. He was defenseless. He had thrown away his knife. He put his hand to his hip, to make sure.

128

'No!' he said aloud.

'What's that?' said Mr Bostock, who had set Michael down. The small boy was already making for home, walking disconsolately, a pathetic little figure.

Robert was startled.

'I said no,' he covered up. 'We can't find it.'

He must not say more, for further pretense would lead to deliberate lying, and he had not yet gone as far as that.

'It's very odd,' said Mr Bostock. 'Who'd have thought a suckling of that age would get right away.'

He pondered on this as they walked slowly homeward, behind the sad little boy. Then he suddenly thought of his daughter.

'But where's Jenny?' he demanded. 'Where did she get to?'

Robert was shaken by another spasm of discomfort. Yes, indeed, where was Jennifer; and what might she have found?

'Oh, she had my bike. She'll have got home by now.'

It was a good guess. They found Jennifer with her mother in the kitchen. She had left Robert's bicycle leaning by the gate in the front garden. He put it away in the barn before following his father and Michael into the house. That took him some minutes, for he moved slowly. He was thinking; and thinking heavily, under a great burden of misgiving. There are times when one's mind can weigh as much as a mountain.

Oddly enough, when he rejoined the family in the kitchen, he found the tension to be over. Michael appeared to have thrown off his misery. After all, his mother and father were happy people together. They were sure and certain, and made no fuss, either one way or the other.

So Mrs Bostock now took Michael's trouble calmly. She could not comfort him in her arms again, because she was making the pastry for a fruit pie, and was up to the elbows in flour.

'What do you say, Father?' she said, perhaps a little too loudly, as though acting a part on the stage of a theater.

'Don't you think that a puppy would like to live in this house?'

'A puppy?' cried Jennifer, quick to take her cue.

'Yes, Mr Culverton told me that the housekeeper's corgi has had three babies, and he offered to buy one for us. He said it would protect us, since we insist on going to bed and leaving all the windows open!'

Robert saw his little brother stir, like a drooping pot plant slowly responding to a can of water. Even the tousled hair took on new life.

'For me?' piped the incredulous voice.

His mother was noticing also. She strengthened the medicine.

'Well, you'd have to look after it yourself; nurse it, feed it, and train it for the house. And no chasing of the sheep, mind you.'

She was leading him further and further away from his recent disaster.

Again, Robert was aware of what his mother intended. He looked at her gratefully, but still mainly on his own account.

As he left the kitchen, he looked back and saw Michael standing at the table, intently listening to his mother while she rolled her pastry. His attention was fastened on every word, as she described the corgi puppies and their superlative beauty. He was not even aware that his hand was picking raspberries waiting in the dish to be covered with the pastry. He did not notice when Mrs Bostock's floury hand gently arrested his and withheld it from the dish, with a pretended slap.

Robert's nervous mind observed this. He told himself that all was well. Michael's devotion had been switched to another object, and a more likely one, practical and lasting.

Robert left his bedroom door open, which was not habitual. He had always been careful to close himself in, wherever he might be; especially in his own lair.

He felt tired out, and sat down on his bed, to stare absently through the window over the small field with the apple orchard beyond. He could see the lowering sunlight rounding the young fruit, so that the apples stood out from the heavy green foliage, clustering close into ripeness.

He sighed with relief. Something was over and done with. He was not sure what it was, for his mind refused to work. He lay back and slept awhile, or half slept, for he could hear a bee buzzing around the room, and the undertone of the myriads of wings in the hot summer air outside. The world was not such a bad place, after all. He was reassured. He thought about Michael, and almost spoke to himself. 'Trust Mother to steer him past *that*!'

He did not think about Jennifer: nor did he see her when she appeared silently at the open door, to stand aside and study him for several moments, before tiptoeing away to her own room at the end of the corridor.

He must really have fallen asleep after that, for when he looked out, the orchard was glowing with the rosy gold of approaching sunset, with the apples even more pronounced on the motherly trees. He got up, washed for dinner, and went downstairs. The house looked different. The world looked different: more solid and friendly.

Mrs Green and Jennifer were setting the table in the dining room.

'Where's everybody?' asked Robert.

Mrs Green looked at him with curiosity, and nodded toward the lawn.

'Why, young man, you look as though you've made a fortune,' she said.

Robert did not take that amiss, as he would have done formerly. He grinned.

'How right you are, Mrs G.,' he replied.

Jennifer, placing the cutlery on the table, looked up but did not speak. She was busy counting the spoons, and getting the sum right.

18 ✤ The Lull before the Storm ✤

Robert found a scene of bliss and peacefulness on the front lawn. Mr Culverton sat in a wicker chair between Mr and Mrs Bostock, all three sipping sherry. The decanter on the stool before them shone like a golden lamp, its flame captured from the sun low in the western sky. Southeast, over the orchard, the disk of the full moon was beginning to thicken to silver.

Robert heard Mr Culverton break the silence.

'Well, a perfect evening, wouldn't you say, Mrs Bostock? Everything serene again? The miracle has worked! Good to be eight years old. Troubles don't last long at that age.'

Robert saw what he was referring to. There, at their feet, sat Michael on the ground, with a corgi puppy between his legs. The tiny creature lay on its back, with its legs stuck stiffly up, while a small hand caressed its stomach. The young lover-naturalist was in heaven again.

'Ah! Robert! Come and see the transformation!'

Mr Culverton raised a hand as he greeted Robert, who squatted down beside Mr Bostock. To his surprise, his father poured half a glass of sherry and handed it to him.

'Here, son. Join us in this pleasure for once. You're still feeling the heat, aren't you?'

Robert took the glass and sipped the wine, wondering what made his father so expansive.

'I'm fine,' he said. 'That chase around was a bit tiring.'

His mother put a finger to her closed lips, and then pointed to the enraptured child sitting with his back to them on the lawn, bent over the puppy.

'We've forgotten all about that,' she said, 'thanks to you, Mr Culverton.'

The visitor ignored this. He was intent on Robert, who felt that massive concentration, and looked up boldly. He was ready for anything, now that life had suddenly become safe.

'I imagined you would be cycling up to do some reading, Robert. I've picked out one or two books that might be worth your attention. You could fit them in with your assigned books, which I gather you've nearly finished?'

Robert thanked him and began to explain why he had not arrived at the castle library, but Mr Culverton cut him short.

'I've heard the story,' he said. 'It explains the new arrival here.' He indicated Michael and the puppy.

'It's a case of all's well that ends well.'

'That's poetry,' said Mr Bostock. 'In real life one thing leads to another, and there's no end to it.'

'Does that apply to your inventions, Bostock?'

'Oh, yes; there's always one improvement ahead, and another beyond that.'

Mrs Bostock stood up, for she had seen Mrs Green appear at the porch.

'But dinner comes first,' she said. 'We're all late tonight, with this endless daylight, and such a happy ending.'

'Don't boast, my dear,' said Mr Bostock. 'There's

still a little time left before midnight, and the moon has to say her piece while we eat. Bob, bring the tray in, will you?'

Michael was persuaded to come in with the rest of the family, and went willingly to bed because, for once, he was allowed to take the corgi up to his room, which adjoined Robert's.

'Bob, leave your door open tonight, for fear the puppy needs attention. I've just put a basket and a piece of blanket beside Mike's bed, and he has promised not to take the little object into bed with him. It would be a bad start. Spoiled dogs are as bad as spoiled children.'

'Don't we know!' said Jennifer, who was already at the table: another concession on this unusual day.

'Puss! Puss!' said Robert, nudging her as he passed. But there was no malice in his teasing. He felt quite kindly toward her; but she ignored him, except for a sidelong glance that might have meant anything.

He did not notice it. For once he was happy. He felt confident and safe. Maybe the half glass of sherry had restored him after that nerve-shaking search, or nonsearch, in the woods. A near thing, he assured himself; a near thing, but all over now. He had the sensation of being grown up, of being included with his parents and Mr Culverton in the talk at the dinner-table. It was great. This was what he had always wanted.

From time to time during the meal and the general conversation, Robert looked across the table at Jennifer. She was behaving demurely on this occasion of her first appearance at late dinner. Sitting beside Mr Culverton, she was a miniature figure, but she was upright and grave, and gave the appearance of being modest and shy. The bulky guest beside her towered benevolently, addressing her with a ceremonious courtesy, as he would a handsome young woman whom he wished to impress.

Robert became somewhat uneasy. There was no need for this. Jennifer's eyes were downcast, except when she looked up and sideways to reply to Mr Culverton. She never once glanced at her brother opposite. He believed she was acting a part, and he was inclined to suspect something.

However, the suspicion passed. The cheerfulness of the dinner party banished it. Mr Culverton was attentive to Robert also, and drew him into the midstream of talk along with Mr and Mrs Bostock, so that he had to keep his wits alert, and not wander off into rather dusty day-dreams, touched with anxiety, as was his habit. After all, there was no need for such moods now. He was sure of that, and told himself so, believing that his narrow escape had made him wiser.

Then, in the midst of the amiable conversation round the dinner table, Jennifer shot one of her arrow-like questions, innocent and deadly.

'Mr Culverton, have you ever seen the ghost that Daddy told us about?'

Silence came down like frost on a bed of flowers.

Robert stared across the table, but he couldn't see Jennifer. For a moment, during the silence, his senses were paralyzed. He was blinded. A spoonful of fruit pie half-way to his mouth stopped, trembling in midair. His hand was cold. He felt the cold in his throat.

'Why do you ask, Jennifer?' said Mr Culverton. His tone was light and easy. It broke the spell. He put his arm along the back of Jennifer's chair and shook her playfully.

'You know, my dear, Deephurst Castle would be lost without its famous ghost! And I would say that people who can't see ghosts are missing a great deal.

There's more in this world than meets the eye. You'd agree with me, eh, Bostock? Where, for instance, do your inventions come from? Explain that to your daughter, if you please!'

Mr Bostock laughed, and handed his plate to Robert, for it to be passed to Mrs Bostock for a second helping of fruit pie.

Robert took it, and saw Jennifer watching his hand as it trembled above the table. He feared the others were watching also, but he could not control the weakness, the cold, the memory of that absurd illusion, which he thought he had dismissed.

He heard his father laugh, and he heard him reply to Mr Culverton, who had so skillfully evaded Jennifer's question.

'I'm an engineer, not a fortune-teller. But there is such a thing as a *hunch*! It usually follows a lot of hard work. That's what your great business organization is paying me for.'

Mr Culverton dropped his light mood, removed his arm from Jennifer's chair, ignored both her and Robert. He leaned forward, and became rocklike; his usual self.

'Bostock! There are thousands of our people working steadily, day by day, year after year. They get along comfortably, though they don't get *hunches*, as you call it. But you do! That's the difference!'

He turned to Jennifer, and also included Robert, who had meanwhile felt the warmth return to his limbs and brain, and some degree of willpower which enabled him to cover up the disturbance made by Jennifer's question. He even noticed that the question remained unanswered by Mr Culverton, who had the last word before Mrs Bostock rose and motioned to Jennifer to lend a hand as Mrs Green came in to clear the table.

'There you are, both of you. You said to me one

day, Robert, that you didn't believe in nonsense. But do your five senses teach you all you want to know, even about *this* world? Think that over, d'you hear me? Think that over!'

He was not angry but he was forceful. At such times he crushed all opposition, without giving a reason. Having spoken, he moved from the dining room, and seemed to leave it empty, though the Bostocks were still there.

'Well, you two?' said Mrs Bostock. 'You've had enough for one summer day. Upstairs, I think! Don't forget to leave your door open, Bob!'

Robert and Jennifer disappeared.

'That fellow sometimes puzzles me,' said Mr Bostock to his wife as he made to follow Mr Culverton out to the garden, and the moonlight. 'See what he makes of my innocent remark about how I get my ideas!'

'Go on with you,' whispered his wife. 'Don't leave your guest out there alone, and take the cigars with you.'

Robert did something he had never done before on his way to bed. He went into Michael's room. Both rooms faced south and the full moon shone through the windows, sending a solid beam of yellowish-blue light, firm as a slab of marble, across the interior. It lay over Michael's bed, and converted the bedclothes, the boy's head and hair, the arm round the puppy, into stone.

Robert studied the sleeping face. It might have been a piece of statuary; so calm, so permanent, in the magical hold of the moonlight. He felt that way himself. Things had worked out well after all, and he was grateful. That, too, was something new.

He remembered his mother's instruction, and he approached the bed, treading lightly. For a moment he hesitated, then he lifted his brother's arm to release the puppy. Michael stirred and muttered in his sleep, 'No!' But nothing more. He fretted a little, then was still.

Robert drew the puppy gently away, and put it in the basket beside the bed. Its head was pillowed on its front paws: no change in posture. The moonlight held the basket, too, in this world of statues.

Robert lingered for a moment, to make sure that Michael did not wake. Then he went to his own room, to find the same transformation there: the beam of moonlight slanted from the window, dividing the room, with the bed highlighted.

While undressing, he saw Jennifer pass the open door, on her way to bed. Funny little creature, he thought. She's still playacting, creeping on tiptoe like that! She raised a hand in passing but did not look his way: or so it seemed in the dim light from a bulb at the stairhead, at the end of the landing.

Robert was uneasy about leaving his door open. He still valued privacy; it was the habit which helped to make him unpopular at school. He closed the door before getting into bed, then realized that he had done so, and got out again to open it. He put a chair against it, for fear a wind should rise in the night, and waken him by slamming it.

Usually, he fell asleep as soon as his head touched the pillow, but tonight he was restless. Maybe the moonlight kept him awake. It was like a solid object across his bed, which he wanted to push away. Also the night was hot, and if he got out again to draw the curtains across, they would rustle and flap behind the open window, no matter how calm the night air.

So he decided to leave it, and turned toward the wall. But still he lay awake. It seemed to be for hours, but that could not be so, for he heard Jennifer creep along the landing again, and she could not have been in bed for so long. He was not sure. She may have forgotten something she had intended to bring up with her.

He did not hear her return, for after that effort to wonder about her, he suddenly fell asleep. Total sleep, for a while.

But his mind could not have been fully at rest, after such a disturbing day. He began to dream, or to believe that he was dreaming. It was a strange condition, a sort of double consciousness, which began with him watching himself tossing and turning in bed, trying to shape words but failing because his mouth was bone-dry, his tongue like a strip of leather.

Then the sense of being two persons died away, and he was himself again. That self must be awake, for he sat up, and saw that the heavy beam of moonlight had shifted from the bed and was now arrested on the wall behind him, in the shape of the window. It reflected from the white paint, cut in two by the exposed oak beam, and sent a suffused light across the room; a dusty, silver atmosphere, through which he peered, still half asleep and dazed. His head felt odd. It ached slightly.

He decided to settle down again, and snuggled his head into the warm pillow, seeking a cooler patch. He was dropping off peacefully, when something disturbed him. He raised his head without sitting up, for he was now really tired.

The sound came from the attic, on the floor above his bedroom. It was faint; a flopping, dragging sound. He did not believe it. He decided to ignore it, and all was quiet again. The whole world was silent, inside the house and out over the countryside.

But there again was the sound. This time it moved right across the attic floor, with interruptions that suggested an intense fatigue. Some effort was being made.

Robert felt the pillow sink under him and he had to exert his neck muscles to prevent his head from dropping back and choking him.

The temperature of the room changed. It was not so much colder as closer. He might be breathing in a tunnel, or an underground passage. But the room was still bright with that misty phosphorescence, for he was now sitting up and staring into it.

Into what?

He was not sure. All he knew was that he felt another presence in the room. He could see it. There, in the dimness of the open doorway, stood, or hovered, the shape which had formed among the bulrushes under the fierce sunlight of the summer afternoon. Now, in the nothingness beyond the glare of the solid moonbeam, it was no different. He saw it at close quarters, the long dark blue coat; the distraught anguish of the skeletal head, still capable of human expression; the raised right arm. Now it pointed not toward the woods where Robert had left the dead piglet covered in bracken waste; it pointed at the chair which he had set against the bedroom door to prevent it from slamming in the night.

Robert tried to speak again, but his mouth was still dry and leathery, and he could make no sound.

But the apparition could. Robert heard it. He heard a human voice right enough, saying something in broken English: yes, with a foreign accent.

'Bury my bones,' it breathed, and repeated the demand several times, in a diminishing tone, as though despairing of any response, retreating and retreating and retreating.

Then it was gone!

Robert was angry. He could not believe what he had seen and heard. He must have been dreaming. He put his hand to his mouth and tried to manipulate his dry lips. Both hand and mouth were cold. His hair damp and matted.

Though he did not believe what had happened, he knew that he could not lie down and sleep until he had looked out along the landing. The sensation was absurd and he knew it.

He was contradicting himself. But there was no help for it. He had to get out of bed and satisfy himself that he had dreamed all this nonsense.

142

He swung his legs out of bed, but the movement was more that of an old man than a boy. His heart beat fast. It might have been that of a wild bird held in his grasp. But he had to satisfy himself. He was conscious of repeating the words silently: 'to satisfy myself', and of course that was what would follow when he looked along the landing.

Those preliminary sounds in the attic meant nothing. There must be a bird up there, or probably a squirrel. Creatures could get in under the eaves of the old building, for there was a great gap between the top of the walls and the overhanging roof trees and tiles.

He was out of bed now, and standing firmly enough. He stepped across the room to the door, but when he reached the chair propped against it, his foot stumbled against some loose object.

It was a spade.

His teeth closed so sharply that his jaws ached. The shock died away, and he found that he was quite calm. Doubts and questionings suddenly vanished, confronted with fact.

The spade had fallen against his hip, where the knife had formerly nestled.

Robert put his hand to it, to prevent it falling further to the floor and rousing the household. For all was silent. The small hours lay over the earth, hushed and moving slowly.

Instantly, on touching the spade, he knew what he must do. He set it gently against the chair, dressed in trousers and coat over his pajamas, pulled on his socks, picked up his shoes and the spade, then crept downstairs. In the scullery he put on his shoes, and left by the unlocked door.

For a few moments he hesitated on the doorstep, on the threshold of the moonlit universe. The silence confronted him, the late summer silence, when birds have finished their singing, and the fearful winter night cries have not yet begun.

But the night was full of perfume, cool and dusty, the scent of ripeness. It encouraged Robert. He no longer felt afraid. Indeed, he accepted the ghost of the French lieutenant as something natural; yes, a part of Nature. There was no question of sense and nonsense. Robert was walking into another world.

He half circled the farmhouse and reached the lane, seeing his way clearly by moonlight. Trees loomed up, more fragile than their shadows, for shadows by moonlight are absolute, dense. One half of the lane was thus cut off by the shadow of the hedgerow on the southern side of it. Robert walked along that invisible half, to ensure secrecy. He must not be seen by anybody, if indeed there were any mortals in this new world into which he had been summoned; the world of the living-dead.

But he was cunning. He knew that this new vision, this new knowledge, new wisdom, into which he had wakened, must at once be put to a practical purpose, like one of his father's 'hunches'. That word had struck in last night at dinner, when Mr Culverton seized on it. Last night? But that was impossible. Time no longer meant anything.

He could not tell how long he had taken to reach the gate; but here he was picking his way across the parkland, a wide ocean of moonlight, silver glinting with dew, and black masses of darkness beside each oak tree.

It was real enough but a different kind of reality. It was like looking at the negative of a photograph. Robert knew what he must do, and therefore he was not afraid, or confused in his mind.

Nor was he alone. Of that he was certain. The

144

French lieutenant was with him, round and about him, even part of himself. Thus he felt that he was two persons come to do the job.

What job?

He knew the answer to that question. There were no hesitations in this strange new world into which he had walked, carrying the spade.

He did not make for the upper lake, though he could see mist lying over its invisible waters, tangled in the bulrushes, like bristles in the moonlight. He headed toward the farther end of the lower lake, past which he had chased Michael's willful little piglet into the closures of the woodland.

When he reached the trees, he was slowed down by the darkness, but he could pick his way by the little medallions of silver light which here and there flickered down through the foliage.

He knew the oak tree, for it was a giant, part of an ancient forest, almost out of place in a modern copse among trimmed sweet-chestnut growth. The kingly old monster stood a little isolated from the rest, as though his subjects were withdrawn, awed and respectful.

Thus the moonlight penetrated there, to add to the regal effect. It also enabled Robert to see what he had to do.

There lay the scattering of bracken which his hand had put down not many hours ago, but in some former lifetime.

He used the spade to remove the bracken. Then he scraped away the damp mass of dead leaves. The small, flesh-colored body of Herbert shone in the shaft of moonlight. Robert, safe in his trance, felt no twinge of fear or disgust. All signs of blood had drained away. The tiny body looked quite holy and pure.

Robert stood motionless above it for some minutes:

but they might as well have been eternity, for much was moving in his mind, some tremendous change of which he was only dimly aware.

He put his hand to his throat, which ached, and to his eyes, which suddenly were blinded. But he quickly wiped away that blindness and got down to work.

He prodded about, seeking here and there for a while and encountering submerged roots. At last he found a patch that offered him clearance for digging a small grave. The soil was light, the top six inches consisting of decayed leaves and twigs, that smelled dank as he moved the humus to get to the earth. That, too, was dark, and still mainly vegetable in texture.

He dug the grave about three feet deep, then paused for breath, realizing that he had worked feverishly. He told himself there was no need for hurry. Time and place around him were canceled out. And this miracle had held him since he obeyed the command of the French lieutenant, whom he could feel near at hand, but no longer visible. The ghost had changed into an idea, and it was an idea of thankfulness. The dreadful stillness of the night sighed with gratitude.

That was how Robert took the tiny breeze that fluttered the leaves of the trees above him, while he picked up the body of the piglet and knelt with it, to lower it into the grave, fragrant with newly-dug earth.

There was no word spoken, for nobody existed except Robert; the French lieutenant had vanished. Robert knew that by instinct, without looking round, or challenging the apparition which had summoned him out into the night on this merciful mission, that was to put things right after deeds of violence, and to bring peace.

He filled in the grave, trod down the soil, and resprinkled humus and the bracken over the raw earth.

Then he left the wood and made his way under the open moonlight, carrying the spade on his shoulder. He did not hurry, for the mood of entrancement was still upon him. But he began to feel a desperate weariness creeping over him. By the time he had crossed the parkland and trudged up the lane to the farm, he could hardly drag one leg after the other. The spade had become so heavy that he left it stuck into a flower bed near the front door of the house. Then he went round to the back.

His task was done.

20 ✤ A New Day Begins ✤

Mrs Bostock was first up next morning. The weather vane on the barn had swung round to the north, and a mist lay over the landscape, dull and damp. The world was so still that all human awakening was belated. That was why Mrs Bostock, expecting her morning tea and not getting it, turned to find her husband still sleeping heavily.

She smiled, recollecting that he and Mr Culverton had sat together at the dining table late last night, talking as men talk when they have interests in common, and passing the decanter.

So she came down alone, and opened the front door, to see what was wrong with the morning. The mist was almost rain, and the lawn was drenched with it. She shivered, and retreated indoors. A pot of tea would be all the more welcome on a day like this.

To her surprise, she found Jennifer in the kitchen. 'What, you awake?' she said.

'Yes, where is everybody?' replied her daughter, yawning. 'Have they all died in the night?'

Mrs Bostock was shocked. 'Jenny! You shouldn't say such things! Really, you are quite uncanny sometimes. You frighten me.'

Jenny apologized. She was devoted to her mother and was almost sorry that Mrs Bostock was not so clever as herself.

148

'I expect we all had too much dinner,' she said. 'Though I woke early enough. It's a bore lying there awake, so I came down to make your tea, but you are up first. Is Daddy asleep?'

'Yes, and I looked in on Michael. The little wretch had got that puppy in bed with him. I hadn't the heart to disturb them. I thought I heard somebody moving about in the night. He must have got out and taken the puppy up.'

'Yes, I expect that's what it was,' said Jennifer demurely. When in that mood, she looked downward, and her extra-long eyelashes covered her eyes with a veil of innocence.

'By the way, there's going to be trouble when your father comes down. Somebody has left a spade out all night and this dampness will rust it up. I saw it from our window. You know what he is! Who could have done that? We did no gardening yesterday evening. Well, I'll go up with our tea. It's time Father bestirred himself.'

She did not notice a sudden flush in her daughter's cheeks.

As soon as she had disappeared upstairs, Jennifer quietly opened the front door and explored outside. There stood the spade, exposed to the weather, leaning against a pillar of the porch. Before she could pick it up, she heard footsteps. Somebody was approaching from the back of the farmhouse. She hesitated, but was too late. Robert appeared.

'Oh, Lord, you look dreadful!' she said. 'Have you had a bad dream or something?'

Robert looked at her. She saw that he was different. He was certainly pale and tousled; but no longer sullen, no longer hostile.

'I couldn't sleep,' he said, but he said it in such a friendly way that Jennifer was startled.

'You're not coming down with something, are you, Bob?' she said.

Before he could reply to this, he saw the spade. The paleness left his cheeks. He flushed, frowned as though trying to recollect something he had forgotten.

'Father will be furious,' he said.

Jennifer saw that he was worried, and worried in a curious way in which he had to be helped.

'No, he won't,' she said quietly. 'He need not know the spade's been left out. Dear old fusspot, he'd go mad if he saw a speck of dirt or rust on one of his precious tools. But you know, he's a genius, Bob. That's how it works.'

'I suppose so,' said Robert dubiously. But he did not contradict her, as formerly he would have done. 'I'll take it back to the toolhouse. I really came down to do just that.'

'No, you won't. You look fagged out, Bob. Go back to bed for a bit, while nobody's about. I'll take it and give it a rub up with one of his oily rags. He'll never know.'

Robert smiled sleepily.

'Bit of a conspiracy, isn't it, Jenny? We've never worked together before, have we?'

'No, and it's rather fun.'

Then she looked at him sharply: one of her characteristic stabs.

'All in a good cause, eh, Bob?'

A touch of the old hostility came back into his eyes as he replied.

'What d'you mean?'

Then it died away again, replaced by a look of appeal, anguished and entreating.

'Bob,' said Jennifer gently, and she leaned toward him as though she wanted to put her arms round him.

But she did not dare do that. 'You said you've come down to put the spade away. So you knew it was there, and who left it there.'

They stared at each other for a long time, and Jennifer saw her brother's face grow whiter and whiter, while his eyes appeared to sink into some cavern of fear. She heard him give a little moan as he collapsed in a dead faint on the lawn, almost at her feet.

Instantly she ran indoors and shouted to her mother to come quickly. Then she ran out, took up the spade and hid it in the shrubs beside the drive. She hurried back to Robert, lifted his head, and slipped her arm round him, as she knelt.

Mrs Bostock appeared, followed by her husband, who leaped forward in front of the mother, fearing something dreadful may have happened.

'What is it? What's been going on?' he whispered, almost angrily to Jennifer, as he knelt at the other side of his son.

She could not reply. Indeed she was not allowed to, for her mother had picked her up, and was half carrying her into the house, while Mr Bostock followed with the unconscious Robert in his arms.

He laid the boy on the couch in the dining room.

'Get a blanket, Jennifer, he's cold,' he said. 'Mary, ring up Culverton. You know he's a medical doctor, though he's never practiced. He'll have remembered enough to be able to stand by until we can get a professional man in from Cranehurst.'

The parents stood, rather helpless, but doing their best by rubbing Robert's hands to keep him warm.

'It's so strange, to happen first thing in the morning! Something uncanny, supernatural, about it!'

As he said that, Mr Bostock took hold of Robert's shoulders, as if determined to drag him back to this world, but the boy still lay unconscious when Mr Culverton arrived, ushered in by the distraught Mrs Bostock.

He said nothing: merely touched Mr Bostock on the back and beckoned him aside. He felt Robert's chest, and lifted an eyelid.

'Some kind of shock,' he said.

'But nothing has happened. We've had a peaceful night. Nothing at all. No, nothing at all!'

Mr Bostock sounded quite angry.

'Is that so?' answered Mr Culverton dryly. There was a long pause, during which Robert stirred, sighed, and opened his eyes. His mouth worked convulsively, then he managed to speak to Jennifer, who had refused to leave his side.

'Have you put it away?' he whispered.

She did not answer. She merely nodded, and touched his cheek, after a swift glance to right and left, to make sure that nobody had overheard.

Mr Culverton now took over. He picked Robert up and sat him in an armchair by the fireplace.

'A hot cup of tea, Mrs. Bostock, I think.'

'It's upstairs,' she said, crying with relief, 'I'll fetch it.'

At the door, she was confronted by a small figure in pajamas, holding a corgi puppy protectively in his arms.

Robert saw him, and smiled wanly, but when he spoke, his voice was firm enough, and friendly enough.

'Hello, kid! You've got the little beast with you!'

There was no need to fetch the doctor from Cranehurst. Half an hour later Robert was himself again, sitting at the breakfast table with the family and Mr Culverton who, being a bachelor, was glad to be included in such a happy party, with the sunlight struggling through the mist and promising another glorious summer day.

Yes, Robert was himself again: at least, not so much *again*, as for the first time in his life, as though something which had puzzled him, baffled him, held him down and almost crushed him, had been explained, exorcized, removed.

And nobody asked any questions; not even when Jennifer left the table, went out to the garden, and was seen to disappear into the shrubbery, on some mission of her own.